"I've never [text obscured by barcode] **"**

She paused b[...] case.
For believing [...]
when I wasn't even sure I believed myself. It's a lot, and I was up half the night thinking I'm kind of awful for not saying this sooner."

The idea they'd both been awake last night but not together made him sad.

"Are you usually this involved in your cases?"

Austin frowned. She couldn't mean what he thought she meant. Could she? "No. Not like this."

He'd never once been attracted to a client. Never wanted to get to know them personally or have them in his life. He'd always done his best to help, nothing more.

There had just been something about Scarlet from the start. And the more he'd gotten to know her, the more he wanted to know. The more he wanted her to stay when this was over. Which was what he should be saying to her right now.

But the risk could outweigh the potential gain.

ALWAYS WATCHING

——

Julie Anne Lindsey

Recycling programs for this product may not exist in your area.

ISBN-13: 978-1-335-59130-2

Always Watching

Harlequin Enterprises ULC
22 Adelaide St. West, 41st Floor
Toronto, Ontario M5H 4E3, Canada
www.Harlequin.com

Printed in U.S.A.

Julie Anne Lindsey is an obsessive reader who was once torn between the love of her two favorite genres: toe-curling romance and chew-your-nails suspense. Now she gets to write both for Harlequin Intrigue. When she's not creating new worlds, Julie can be found carpooling her three kids around northeastern Ohio and plotting with her shamelessly enabling friends. Winner of the Daphne du Maurier Award for Excellence in Mystery/Suspense, Julie is a member of International Thriller Writers, Romance Writers of America and Sisters in Crime. Learn more about Julie and her books at julieannelindsey.com.

Books by Julie Anne Lindsey

Harlequin Intrigue

Beaumont Brothers Justice

Closing In On Clues
Always Watching

Heartland Heroes

SVU Surveillance
Protecting His Witness
Kentucky Crime Ring
Stay Hidden
Accidental Witness
To Catch a Killer

Visit the Author Profile page at Harlequin.com.

CAST OF CHARACTERS

Scarlet Wills—A real estate agent in Marshal's Bluff, North Carolina, being followed and tormented by an unknown individual.

Austin Beaumont—A private investigator who will stop at nothing to protect Scarlet from her stalker and help bring the criminal into custody.

Dean Beaumont—A private investigator and business partner with Austin, working hard to assist his brothers and local law enforcement in finding and stopping Scarlet's stalker.

Lydia Stevens—A friend of Scarlet and fellow real estate agent in the Coulter Realty office, Marshal's Bluff location.

Trina Wills—Scarlet's mother, a seasoned real estate agent in a neighboring county.

Mrs. Beaumont—The Beaumont family matriarch, who runs a restorative ranch with her husband and champions the interests of her five grown sons.

Detective Finn Beaumont—A Marshal's Bluff detective working with his brothers and local police to identify and capture Scarlet's stalker.

Officer Barrow—A police officer in Trina Wills's town, who responds to her disappearance and works with the Marshal's Bluff police to locate Trina and the stalker.

Cindy Reese—A real estate agent in Trina Wills's office.

Chapter One

Scarlet Wills paced the empty living room of the moderately priced two-story home on Wentworth Drive, hands clutched before her, heart rate on the rise. Thanks to a recent overhaul of the outdated Coulter Realty website, house hunters could now request a walk-through of any available property by completing an online request form. Scarlet had assumed this new feature would lead to an increase in appointments, showings, clients and sales. She hadn't, however, considered the lack of personal interaction meant never really knowing who was on the other side of the requests.

The contact form required only a name, phone number or email address, and the home a buyer wanted to see. Half the time, Scarlet didn't know who she was meeting until they'd arrived. Other times, like this one, no one arrived at all.

She rolled her tight shoulders and leaned her head side to side, hoping to alleviate the painful tension gathered there. This was beginning to look like Scarlet's third no-show in the five weeks since Coulter Realty's website changes went live.

And, like the other times, she felt distinctly as if she was being watched.

She'd breathed easier when she'd first arrived, glad to see another agent already at the home with a couple of potential buyers. Evan's familiar face and ready smile had been a welcome surprise. He'd even complimented her short-sleeved navy blouse and the way she'd worn her pale blond hair in a tight chignon. But now, he and his clients were leaving, and she would be alone.

According to her watch, it was nearing six o'clock. Hardly late, but the sky was already dark when she'd pulled her compact SUV into the long driveway. Autumn in her small coastal town of Marshal's Bluff, North Carolina, meant eating dinner after dark for more than a few months of the year. And Wentworth Drive was heavily lined with trees, the homes cloaked in shadows.

Ideally, Scarlet's potential client would've shown up before Evan left, but that, apparently, wasn't meant to be.

Now, she paced alone inside the eerily quiet structure, watching helplessly as gooseflesh climbed the exposed skin of her arms and Evan said goodbye to his clients on the lawn outside the dining room's bay window.

He waved a hand as his clients drove away, and Scarlet willed him to return inside. But he dropped into his car without another look in her, or the home's, direction.

A heavy, shuddered sigh escaped her as she checked her watch again. Pat Cranston, the contact who'd reached out to her, was officially more than fifteen minutes late, and her nerves were beginning to fray.

She refocused on the scene outside the window. October was once her favorite month of the year. The beauty that came with changing leaves and blooming mums was unparalleled. And her small coastal town thrived on harvest festivals, pumpkins patches and gratuitous, multicolored gourds on every doorstep.

Currently, however, it was hard to see past the early sunsets and shorter days. There was too much darkness and there were too many shadows.

Too much paranoia, she thought, chastising herself for the continued fixation on something unseen. Something that likely wasn't even real.

Moving to Marshal's Bluff four years ago had been an easy decision. She'd grown up in a neighboring county, where her mother, Trina, was a successful real estate agent. And in small-town North Carolina, one Wills woman selling homes was enough. In Marshal's Bluff, she didn't have to compete with her mother for home sales, and no one referred to her as Trina's daughter. Two big bonuses of setting up shop an hour away.

She stared at her SUV for long minutes, debating on when she could reasonably call it a night.

Soon the grandfather clock in the foyer gonged, and Scarlet's green eyes widened in the reflection of the glass. It was definitely time to give up and head home.

Pat hadn't responded to any of Scarlet's texts attempting to confirm the appointment, and twenty minutes was more than enough grace time on Scarlet's part. Besides, she had a bottle of merlot, an excellent book and set of new satin pajamas just waiting for her at home.

She began the process of shutting off lights at the back of the home and moving forward, careful not to leave any unnecessarily on, extra grateful Evan had turned off the upstairs and basement lights before he'd left. Scarlet double-checked the locks on all exterior doors, then paused to collect her business cards and flyers she'd printed with details on the home and local market.

It really was a pretty home. Only three years old and full of modern charm. High ceilings. White woodwork and trim. Fancy, geometric-shaped light fixtures and marble everywhere marble was acceptable. Not her style, but lovely nonetheless.

The rooms, though flawlessly designed, were mostly empty now, thanks to a relocation that had taken the family to another state more than a week prior. Another similarity, she realized, in the homes where she'd been stood up. The appointments were always made online. Always for a home with limited neighbors and a family no longer in the area.

Her phone buzzed, and she flinched before rolling her eyes belatedly at the overreaction. The name of another client living out of state appeared on her caller ID.

"Good evening, Mr. Perez," she said sweetly, thankful for the bit of normal in her current situation. "How are you tonight?"

"Not good," he griped. "You assured me you could sell my house in a week, and it's been a month."

Scarlet headed into the foyer, tugging her purse onto one shoulder. "No, Mr. Perez," she corrected pleasantly. "I said I could sell your house in a week at the listing price I suggested. I told you I would do my best to sell your home at the price you insisted upon."

"I don't see the difference."

She highly doubted that. He was a businessman after all. And she'd explained the difference to him more than once. *Still*, she reasoned, *it would be nice to keep him on the phone a little longer.* "Your price is significantly higher than I recommended, which limits the number of prospective buyers. That's not to say the property won't sell at your price. I'm confident you can get the amount you're asking, but it won't happen as quickly. We're going to have to wait for the right buyer."

She stepped into the night and locked the door behind her. A cool breeze whipped the fabric of her blouse, sending a sharp chill down her spine. "If you can be patient a little longer, I'll brainstorm new ideas for spreading the word on a larger scale."

He grunted. Not happy, but not angry. With Mr. Perez, she'd call that a win.

Scarlet stilled as motion caught her eyes in the reaching shadows along the roadside. She stared and squinted into the darkness, begging the vague, sweeping movement to grow into something recognizable and harmless. A neighbor walking a dog, or a few wandering deer.

"I don't have forever on this," Mr. Perez complained. "My family's move was expensive, and we can't afford to pay two mortgages long term."

Scarlet made a break for her little SUV, racing down the steps and across the black asphalt drive-way toward her vehicle. The lights flashed when she pressed the unlock button on her key fob. "Give me two more weeks to find a buyer at this price," she suggested. "Then we can revisit the subject of pricing."

"All right," he agreed reluctantly. "Two more weeks. But I want it sold. At my price."

"Understood."

She slid behind the wheel and dropped the phone into her cup holder, enjoying the satisfying snap of her power locks as the door closed. A few frantic heart-beats later, she reversed carefully away from the dark, empty home.

She queued up an audiobook at the nearest intersec-tion, obeying a stop sign. A pair of headlights flashed on behind her, pulling her attention to the blinding reflection in her rearview mirror. Unfounded tension coiled through her limbs. "It's just a car," she whis-pered, pressing the gas pedal once more.

It didn't make any sense to assume the car was in-tentionally following her, so she motored on, shaking away the nonsensical thoughts. For good measure, she pressed the gas pedal with purpose, putting extra space between the vehicles.

Her company's online request form for house showings popped back into her mind. As did her three no-shows. Was it ridiculous to wonder if those requests had been made by the same person? Even if the names and contact numbers were different?

Above her an abundance of stars twinkled in an inky sky. Behind her, the glow of headlights grew until she had to look away. The other vehicle erased the distance she'd gained then crept uncomfortably closer before matching her speed.

Scarlet's grip on the wheel tightened, and she worked a little harder to convince herself the car wasn't following her and the driver wasn't trying to unsettle her. Whoever was back there probably always drove like a jerk, too close and too fast. It had nothing to do with her. She accelerated anyway, reaching nearly sixty miles per hour in the stretch of road marked forty-five. She'd cheerfully accept the speeding ticket if it meant seeing a cop anytime soon. At least then the car behind her would be gone, and if she played her cards right, the officer might willingly follow her home for good measure.

She decided to drive into town to be safe instead of heading straight home. As the downtown lights came into view on the horizon, she made a mental plan. She'd drive into the busiest parking lot and call a friend. If the car followed, she'd call the police. If the car went away, she'd wait five minutes, then take a roundabout and convoluted path home to be sure no one else was behind her when she arrived.

Paranoid? Maybe. But at least she had a plan.

She pulled her phone into her lap for good measure. If anything else happened, if the car hit her or the driver got out at the upcoming stoplight and moved in her direction, she would dial 911.

Her attention fixed on the rearview mirror as she slowed. The car picked up speed, and she braced for impact, until it suddenly peeled away, taking the exit ramp for the highway instead of stopping at the light.

Breath whooshed from her lungs, and a ragged laugh burst from her trembling lips. "Good grief," she whispered. "I'm losing it."

The other driver had simply been a jerk in a hurry to get somewhere, and she'd been prepared to call emergency services. For what? Tailgating? Clearly she needed a good night's sleep more than she'd thought.

When the light turned green, she drove straight home.

SCARLET SLID INTO bed that night with a glass of red wine and her favorite novel. A long, hot shower had washed the fear from her mind. "Just one chapter," she vowed. "Then it's bedtime."

She lifted the glass to her lips, and her cell phone vibrated, announcing an incoming message before she'd taken a single sip.

She didn't recognize the name, but that wasn't unusual. She'd printed her cell phone number on her business cards and shared it on the company website. Also, the new contact form pushed requests for home showings to their assigned agents via text.

She set her wine aside and raised the device reluctantly, hoping it was someone interested in the Perez property and willing to pay his asking price. She accessed the message with a swipe of her thumb.

Unknown: Nice seeing you again tonight

Not an offer on the Perez place, but at least it was a wrong number.

The phone buzzed a second time before she could return it to the nightstand.

Scarlet stilled, eyes fixed on the four little words.

Unknown: Thanks for the showing

Breath caught in her throat. Was it possible this too was a coincidence? A message meant for another agent? A confused buyer texting the wrong number from the website?

Or was this the point where she could no longer tell herself there wasn't anything to worry about?

A final text made her decision clear.

Unknown: CU soon

Chapter Two

Austin Beaumont leaned against the darkly tinted window at the front of his office, watching morning traffic creep along outside. His simple T-shirt and jeans reflected in the glass, as did the mug of coffee in his hands.

Every shop on the street had dragged out their autumn decor, complete with piles of pumpkins on hay bales and scarecrows with goofy grins. Even the private detective firm he owned with his older brother Dean had a bundle of cornstalks outside the door and a wreath of multicolored leaves with a Welcome sign. Not exactly the intimidating, highly serious, let us take your case vibe he imagined for his business, but there wasn't any use saying no to their mother. She insisted on making everyone comfortable.

She'd arrived with decor and a dinner invitation three weeks back. He'd declined the former and accepted the latter, but received both instead. The upside to his loss, he supposed, was the likelihood of making potential clients feel less on edge and more welcome. In his experience, when someone contacted a private investigator, they'd already made up their mind about getting help. He'd prefer his firm got the job.

A small SUV appeared in the curb lane, slowing by a fraction, then bouncing gently ahead. The warped brick streets of downtown Marshal's Bluff weren't built to handle the recent influx of vehicles. But a tax reduction for businesses had drawn the attention of several companies with ties to national corporations, which meant the town's population was experiencing a boom.

"What are you looking at?" Dean asked. The sounds of his brother's fingers on his keyboard underscored the words.

Austin peered over his shoulder at Dean's amused expression, and his partner stilled.

"What is it?"

"A dark SUV has passed here twice. It slows outside, then continues each time."

"What are you thinking?" Dean asked. "Lost commuter or possible trouble?"

Austin shrugged, maintaining the carefully disinterested facade he preferred to the tightly wound, barely suppressed, ball of tension he was. He'd perfected the act in the military and found it worked wonders in civilian life as well. People who looked cool and confident bred trust and put others at ease, exactly what a businessman wanted and what a calculating investigator needed. Being underestimated, or even overlooked, was often a golden ticket in his work.

He sipped his cooling coffee, which had become more of a prop than it had been when he'd poured it.

Then flashed his brother a smug half smile. "Given the amount of criminals and cheating spouses we help bust every month, I'm hoping it's not the latter."

"That makes both of us," Dean said, doubling down on whatever he was up to on the computer.

The click-clacking of keys only lasted another minute before the office phone rang, and Dean's voice rose again. "Beaumont Investigations."

Austin returned the mug to his desk and grabbed a black ball cap from his bottom drawer.

The office was wide and rectangular, with two desks out front, bookshelves, chairs and other homey touches their mother had insisted upon. Two small conference rooms lined a corridor leading to the private employee section, where they kept a well-stocked kitchenette for long hours at the office and stakeouts.

Austin tugged the hat over his shaggy, sandy brown hair, reminding himself again to get a trim, and adjusted the bill low on his forehead. Then he strolled out the front door. He walked along the sidewalk to the end of the block and around the corner.

Brisk morning air swept along the streets between historic brick buildings, stirring up fallen leaves and setting a discarded plastic bag into flight.

He leaned casually against the wall at his back. The position of the building compared to the morning sun created a long shadow where he was likely to go unnoticed. He lowered his head, as if enraptured by his cell phone, just in case he caught a passerby's eye.

As predicted, the SUV reappeared, making its turn onto the street before him. And in a stroke of luck, the light at the corner turned red. Unfortunately, the same sun that had helped him blend into the shade, cast a bright glint off the vehicle's windshield, making it impossible to get a good look at the driver.

Austin murmured a curse and revised his plan. Better to know what he was dealing with than to be unprepared. He pushed away from the wall and strode into traffic, crossing the single narrow lane of moving cars with ease. He stopped on the yellow lines at the road's center and rapped his knuckles against the lightly tinted driver's-side window.

Clouds passed over the brilliant North Carolina sun, removing the glare from the glass and enabling him to get his first look at the driver, just as she screamed.

His hands flipped up in innocence, and he took in the shock and horror on the woman's beautiful face. Her pale green eyes flashed with fear, then red-hot anger.

"I'm calling the police!" she yelled, turning her phone to face him as if snapping a picture.

Austin reared back, stunned and a little amused, but earning a honk from an oncoming car. He raised a hand in apology to the vehicle, then returned to the double yellow lines.

When his eyes met hers again, the woman pointed pepper spray at her closed window, cell phone at her ear.

A hearty laugh rumbled unexpectedly from his chest, opening his lips into a wide smile. The light changed, and the SUV rolled away. He waited for a break in traffic then jogged back to the sidewalk at his first opportunity.

He took a minute to remove his hat and run a hand through his hair before securing the cap once more. And another minute to press back the smile still twisting the corners of his mouth.

"I am clearly Marshal Bluff's top investigator," he muttered, shaking his head as he made his way around the corner. Dean would never let him live this one down if he told him what had happened, and the story was too ridiculous not to share.

Instead of saving their office from an attack by a disgruntled criminal or cheater looking for retribution, he'd scared some poor, obviously rattled woman half to death, and nearly gotten a face full of pepper spray for his trouble.

With a little luck, she wouldn't panic and send that photo to the local police station. For starters, that would be terrible for business. And on a personal note, his younger brother, and Marshal's Bluff detective, Finn would surely print and hang the image on every telephone pole between Main Street and the coast.

He'd been certain the vehicle was paying special interest to the office as it passed. But maybe the driver really was lost, and he was losing his touch. He normally sensed trouble from a mile away, sometimes before the person who'd eventually cause the issue even knew that was the path they were on.

He shook out his hands, which had balled uncharacteristically into fists, curled by the tension and distaste of such a total error. He wouldn't blame her if she did call the police. A stranger had approached her in traffic. A guttural sound rumbled low in his chest as Beaumont Investigations came into view. Time to pull it together and focus on the full day he had ahead of him. Vandalism investigations. A stolen stallion worth more than his truck. An allegation of hidden funds amidst a divorce dispute. And those were the tip of the iceberg.

Hopefully the call Dean had taken before Austin went outside to confront an unsuspecting woman was information on one of those cases. Anything to set his day back on course.

A gust of coffee-scented air rushed out to greet him as he pulled open the glass office door. His mother's festive leaf wreath swung wildly under the force.

The SUV driver's face flashed into his mind unbidden. She'd been angry and afraid, but beautiful, with the soft green eyes and plush pink lips of an angel. Maybe it was the morning he was having, or the way his instinctual sense of dread refused to let up, but he couldn't help wondering what had upset her. Why had she been circling the block?

Probably a marital squabble, he told himself. Women who looked like that didn't stay single. Even if she had the personality of a viper. Though he doubted that was true. She'd seemed vulnerable. And unnaturally quick to raise her pepper spray. Everyone else in town greeted neighbors, and strangers, with a smile and a nod.

He rubbed a hand against the back of his neck and gave one last glance through the window before meeting Dean's curious stare.

"Everything okay?"

"Yep." Austin fell onto his desk chair as Dean rose from his.

"Good." He tugged on his brown leather coat and reached for his cell phone and keys. "Finn called. He's got some information on my missing person's case. I'm headed to the police station to check it out."

Austin nodded, attention fixed on his now tepid coffee. "That was Finn on the phone when I left?" He stretched upright again, in need of caffeine and something to busy his hands.

"No, that was a potential new client, which is why it's good there isn't a disgruntled nut casing this place. I have to take off, and you can handle the client. I've already opened a file and logged the basic information. It's in the shared drive. Give it a read before she gets here."

Austin shut his eyes for a long beat to stop them from rolling. This was hardly his first rodeo, yet something about the older brothers in his family made them think the younger brothers always needed help. Guidance. Or pointers. It wasn't personal, but it was habitual, and he made another mental note not to do the same to Finn and Lincoln. Besides, Dean's sage advice to be prepared was Scouts and cowboy 101. Austin had passed those life courses with gold stars years ago.

He forced himself to refocus on the more important information Big Brother failed to provide. "When's this woman getting here?" And did he have time to pour a fresh cup of coffee? "What's her name and problem?"

"Scarlet Wills, twenty-seven, unmarried, lives alone.

Thinks she's being followed," Dean said, narrowing his eyes. "Read the file."

Austin frowned and headed for the coffee maker.

His brother moved toward the door.

The bell dinged, and Dean spoke again, but he didn't say goodbye.

"Ms. Wills?"

Great. She was already there. Austin's head fell forward on an exhale, and he straightened with resolve. No hot coffee for him then.

He forced a polite expression and turned back toward his desk as Dean shook the newcomer's hand.

"I'm Dean Beaumont. This is my brother and business partner, Austin Beaumont. He'll be meeting with you today and getting a feel for your situation. He's military trained, the middle-born of five rowdy brothers and an Eagle Scout. Not to mention he makes a mean cup of joe. You've never been in better hands, I assure you."

Dean's smile was warm and charming as he did his best to break the ice and put Ms. Wills at ease before walking out.

But her wide green eyes were already fixed on him in recognition, and Austin blew out a long, defeated breath. Hopefully the gorgeous blonde before him, the one he'd unintentionally startled in her SUV, would give him a chance to explain before making use of that pepper spray, wherever it was now.

He was definitely going to need that coffee.

Chapter Three

Scarlet froze as Dean Beaumont, the man she'd spoken to on the phone, walked away. Leaving her with his brooding brother. Dean had been kind and polite in person, and for a moment, the mounting tension inside her had faded. It probably helped that he was distractingly handsome. Unfortunately, she never went for the happy, congenial sort. One of her many flaws. Just ask her mother.

Not to ruin her perfect record of bad luck with men, she'd managed to threaten the private detective in front of her with pepper spray. The same man whose help she needed to figure out if there really was a stalker to worry about. Worse? Austin Beaumont looked exactly like the kind of guy she'd cheerfully hitch her wagon to, then get burned.

She scanned the room as he assessed her, taking the opportunity to gather her thoughts and resolve. The office was nicely decorated, with bookshelves and framed photos. Two mahogany desks faced the large front window and glass door, each with a leather executive chair behind it and two padded armchairs before it. The air was warm and smelled of delectable cologne and coffee.

"Ms. Wills," he said finally, tossing his black ball cap onto a shelf and running a hand through his shaggy brown hair. The soft locks fell over his forehead as he moved forward with an outstretched arm.

Manners lifted her hand to his before her brain had made the conscious decision to do so. "Please, call me Scarlet."

The air thickened and tingled between them as his calloused palm curled over hers. The heat from his touch sent sparks of attraction up her arms and into her chest.

He was unfairly handsome without his hat to shield his features, but not at all like his brother. Dean had been light and jovial. Austin had an air of danger around him. His dark, hooded gaze should've felt more like a warning than an invitation.

"I should apologize for frightening you earlier," he said.

Not actually apologizing, she noted and released his hand with some mental effort.

"And I should apologize for threatening you."

His lips quirked in amusement, without quite forming a smile. "Can I get you a cup of coffee?"

"Please."

"You can have a seat, if you'd like." He motioned to the desk on her left, then moved into a narrow hallway beyond the outer office where she stood. "I won't be a minute."

Unnerved by a torrent of emotions, from fear and

hope to attraction and anxiety, she remained fixed in place. What did she hope would happen today? What would the PI say about her concerns? She certainly didn't want her fears confirmed, but hearing the danger was all in her imagination didn't seem ideal either. What would that mean about the state of her emotional health?

She bypassed the desk and chairs for a look at the bookshelves and photos. Images of the men she'd just met were accompanied by a collection of other friendly faces. A group shot included the PIs and three other men, roughly the same ages, each with a dauntingly attractive face. An older couple shared an embrace in the background. The Beaumont family?

Smaller frames featured individuals that looked nothing alike. All ages, with a variety of hair and eye colors and skin in every tone from ivory to ebony.

The top shelf held a shadow box with a Purple Heart medal and a dozen images of men in military uniforms or fatigues. A younger version of Austin leaned against a tank. Sweat had applied the cotton of his plain white T-shirt to every perfect muscle and plane of his chest like a sticker. Tan and brown camouflage-patterned pants and black boots completed the ensemble. A sheen of sweat was visible on his brow.

"Cream or sugar?" a low male voice asked, snapping Scarlet back to the moment.

She spun to find Austin barely three feet away, steam rising from the mug in each hand.

"No. Thank you."

He set the drinks on the desk and took a seat. "See anything interesting?"

"Just looking at all these faces," she said, demanding her traitorous gaze not return to the lucky white T-shirt. "You're from a military family?"

"I am."

"Is the Purple Heart yours?" Her voice cracked unexpectedly, and she cleared her throat. Something about the idea of Austin being wounded pressed the air from her lungs.

"No. That belongs to my youngest brother. He had it rough for a while and wasn't interested in keeping the medal around."

"But you were?"

Austin's brows lifted by a fraction, probably making a note of her nosiness. "I think that medal is a symbol of his survival. Not everyone who earns one lives to see it. I plan to honor and protect it until he's ready to take it back."

She wet her lips and swallowed. This man had heart. If the photos weren't enough to make things crystal clear, his speech had driven the message home. Austin Beaumont had served his country, and he clearly loved his family. Her crush on him was inevitable now. "And all these framed photos of children..." She looked at the images again. All so vastly different. Missing persons he and his brother helped locate? "Kids you helped bring home?"

"I'm afraid that credit goes to my folks," he said. "Those are my brothers and sisters."

Her smile sprouted. "Really? All of them?"

Austin rose and joined her at the bookshelves. "My parents run a ranch where they help troubled young people. They also foster and adopt. Most of these are grown now." He tipped his head toward the photos. "Some were adopted by other families, others aged out of the system, but for at least a little while they were raised by my folks. That makes them siblings for the long haul in my book."

A new warmth spread through her chest, and she turned to him. "Family dinners must be interesting."

"You have no idea."

She didn't, but she would love to. "There are five boys in your immediate family. How many were adopted?"

"Two," he said, stretching a hand in the direction of his desk. "We should get started."

"Oh." She'd nearly forgotten why she was there. "Right."

He hadn't clarified which of his brothers had been adopted, or if he was one of them, but it was clear that didn't matter.

Her heart gave another thud of appreciation.

She returned to the gray armchair in front of his desk. She'd always dreamed of having siblings, but it must've been hard to watch them come and go.

Austin sipped his coffee then moved the wireless mouse in a quick circle, waking up the computer. A moment later, he typed something with the keyboard. "Dean opened a file for you. I'm going to add additional information as we talk."

"Okay." Scarlet rested her hands in her lap, kneading her fingers to stall her nerves. "I'm hoping I'll laugh about this later," she said, planting both feet against the floor. She cursed the unforgiving pencil skirt she'd chosen for the day, unable to cross her legs and bounce her knee as she wanted. The material was too snug and short to make the move smoothly, and a second-rate flashing would be nearly as humiliating as having threatened the man with her pepper spray.

His trained gaze slid over her features and hair, along the length of her neck and torso to her hands. Probably sensing her thoughts and tension. "There's no need to be nervous. You're the one with the weapon."

A soft, unexpected snort of laughter broke on her lips, and her cheeks heated. "I guess you really can read my mind."

"Is that what you think?"

"Don't you know?"

The skin at the corners of his eyes crinkled with mischief, and his lips formed a lazy half smile.

She pushed the moment of lightness aside and hoped her imagined stalker wasn't any more real than mind reading. "I should probably start from the beginning."

She told the story as well as possible with the intensity of Austin's gaze on her, starting with an explanation of the company's website upgrade and her many calls to tech support, because attempting to navigate the system's changes was a low point in her recent career. She moved on to describe the three requests for home showings that had resulted in no-shows and carefully outlined the similarities. She included the homes' locations and absent owners. For her grand finale, she told him about the texts.

"May I see the messages?" he asked.

Scarlet unearthed the phone from her structured leather handbag and unlocked it with her fingerprint before accessing the texts. "The number doesn't match the one given on the contact form from last night. I checked as soon as the shock passed. It also doesn't match the number used for either of the other appointments when no one showed. Which is why I hope I'm overthinking all this."

"Burner phones are cheap and widely available." Austin took the device. His expression hardened as he read the messages but cleared before he raised his eyes to hers once more. "I'd like to take screenshots as evidence."

"Of course." Scarlet nodded woodenly and cringed inwardly at his word choice. Evidence made it sound as if he believed there was enough reason to open a case. As if she was already in the midst of a criminal investigation. "Do you really think someone would go to all that trouble to upset me? Using multiple numbers and sending me on three goose chases just to watch me roam around empty homes?"

Austin caught her in his dark gaze once more, jaw set and expression firm. "What do your instincts say?"

She blew out a slow sigh, deflating against the chair's backrest. She wouldn't be in his office if she could've found a way to let the suspicions go on her own.

"Instincts are rarely wrong," he said, apparently reading the answer in her body language. "People ignore their guts too often, especially women who tend to be more concerned about manners than men. Statistically you're more likely to be in danger of attack or abduction than I am and less likely to be able to fight off your attacker. That alone is reason not to take chances." He tapped the screen a few times then set her phone on his desk between them. "I would encourage you to walk away from anyone and any situation that makes you feel uncomfortable, even if you aren't sure why. Just turn around and leave. As far as these contact forms go, I'd tell your company it's an unsafe practice and you aren't showing homes to anyone else you don't meet in advance, at least by phone. Whatever you need to feel safe."

Scarlet considered his words and her situation for a moment, a new concern itching in her mind. "The contact form has only been in effect for five weeks. If someone is doing this, could they have been one of the first buyers I met through the site, then used the same method to make additional appointments?"

Austin leaned forward on his desk, appearing to weigh his response before giving it. "It's possible someone was watching you before the website changed, and once they realized the new contact form gave them direct access to you, they began to take advantage. He might even see these appointments as dates. Or think you're buying a house together."

Her stomach plummeted and the downy hairs on her arms and neck rose to attention. "You think someone could've been following me, watching me, for more than five weeks?"

"I think anything is possible," he said. "And if last night was the first time he's contacted you afterward, I think he's escalating."

Her mouth opened, and she snapped it shut. Escalating. There was another word she didn't like. A word that made her blood run cold.

"Is there anything else?" he asked. "Even if it's small, it could matter. Even things from before the website gained a request form? Things you dismissed at the time that might look more pointed now."

She shook her head, prepared to insist nothing else had happened, outside the texts and no-shows. Then something flashed back to mind. "Someone followed me last night when I left the home on Wentworth." She told the story slowly and in detail, watching Austin carefully for a reaction.

His jaw clenched and released several times before he spoke. "Can you describe the car?"

"Not really. It was dark, and I was shaken. I'm sure it was a car though, not a truck or SUV. Black or another dark color, I think. With those bluish headlights."

"That's good," he said, voice soothing and certain. "All those details will help if we come to need them."

Her tension eased by a fragment. She wasn't a confirmed victim yet, but if her fears did come true, she wanted to be useful.

"I'd like to look into this further," he said. "I have some things to tie up and off-load this morning, but I want to get started as soon as possible."

"Tomorrow?" she asked, both thankful and concerned by his decision to take her case.

"I was thinking I could meet you at your office after work today. Maybe interview your coworkers. Meanwhile, I'll check out the company website and do a little reconnaissance at the homes where you felt watched. Can you text me those addresses?" He pulled a sleek black business card from a holder on his desk and slid it in her direction.

She struggled to regain her breath as the reality of things attempted to flatten her to the chair. "You want to meet my coworkers?" She plucked the card from the desk and accepted her cell phone when he passed that to her as well.

"I do, but we can play that however works best for you. Tomorrow, I'd like to begin shadowing you for a day or two. I'll stay in the background. You won't even notice I'm there once we start."

Scarlet highly doubted that. In fact, now that they'd met, she was sure she'd notice him in a stadium full of people. And wasn't one person following her enough? "What do I tell people? My clients?"

He smiled warmly, the picture of calm.

She on the other hand was sure he could hear her erratic heartbeat across the space between them.

"You could tell clients I'm a trainee, if that helps. I'll even wear a suit."

Her mind went fuzzy at the thought of him in dress clothes, the crisp white sleeves of his shirt rolled up to his elbows. "And my coworkers?" she croaked, throat suddenly parched. "I don't want them to know what I'm worried about until I'm sure there's reason for concern."

"Long-lost cousin," he suggested. "New boyfriend? Just let me know what feels right to you."

She swallowed audibly and wished for a bottle of iced water instead of cooling coffee. She took an eager sip anyway. "And your rate?"

"No charge until I know there's a case. We can talk more about it in a day or two."

Scarlet rose and slid her purse strap over one shoulder. "I guess I'll see you tonight. Six o'clock at the Coulter Realty office?"

"I'll be there." Austin walked her to the door and held it open as she passed.

When she buckled into her SUV across the street, he was still watching, and she tried not to stare. His tan, taut body leaned against the exterior wall. Autumn wind ruffled his hair.

Scarlet released a shaky breath and eased away from the curb, feeling the weight of his gaze on her as she passed.

If suspicions of a stalker weren't her complete undoing, the red-hot attraction she'd felt for Austin Beaumont would be.

Chapter Four

Scarlet drove to work feeling significantly lighter than she had when she'd left home, but also a little flushed. Austin Beaumont had put her mind at ease on the potential stalker situation and given her something altogether different to think about until she saw him again. He'd been a consummate professional in his speech and interactions, but something in his eyes had felt downright inviting. An unspoken dare or challenge.

Or maybe she was projecting.

Regardless, it'd been a long time since she'd experienced a physical reaction while speaking to a man. Yet, as she sat in that PI office, her heart had raced and her thighs had clenched. Her mind had even begun to wonder if he was as capable in private matters as he seemed to be in professional ones. More, what would his lips feel like on hers? What did he taste like? And was he open to entertaining her curiosity?

All thoughts she never had. Clearly the recent paranoia was affecting her mind.

She kept an eye on her rearview mirror as she made her way along familiar downtown streets toward the

Coulter Realty offices. No one appeared to be following her, but she still breathed easier when she pulled into the lot behind a coworker. Now she wouldn't have to cross the lot alone.

Lydia Stevens, a newer and younger agent who'd grown up in Marshal's Bluff, climbed out with a grin. A collection of bags hung from her fingertips. Her brown hair was curled into thick beachy waves and hanging loose over her shoulders. The fitted red dress she wore emphasized her runner's figure, and an oversize cream-colored cardigan hung off her narrow frame. She hiked a black laptop bag and a designer purse onto one shoulder then slid a canvas tote and thermal lunch bag into her opposite hand.

Considering the tennis shoes on her feet, Scarlet guessed the canvas tote held Lydia's high heels for appointments. From experience she knew the lunch bag contained a reusable water bottle, a lidded bowl of sliced veggies and a ready-made smoothie or protein shake.

Scarlet admired the ambition, but she stuck with sensible two-inch pumps she could wear comfortably all day. And she ordered lunch on the go, when she had time to eat at all.

Lydia waved as she waited for Scarlet to park and join her. "Hey, you! How was the showing last night? Did you make another sale?"

"No. It was another no-show. My third in five weeks." She considered telling Lydia more about her suspicions and her visit with the local PI, but decided to wait until she knew more. Thinking she had a stalker if she didn't would just make her sound loopy. And telling someone else about her fears would make it all feel more real. Scarlet didn't want either of those things to happen, so she refreshed her smile and locked the car behind her.

Lydia pushed out her bottom lip. "Bummer. So you're still having trouble with the requests from the contact form?"

"Apparently. Have you had any issues?"

"No." Lydia followed her to the office door. "But I don't get a lot of requests that way yet. I'm still too new. I think the system checks senior agents' calendars first. So I only get the lead if everyone else is busy."

Scarlet paused to open and hold the door for her colleague to pass. "Do you ever get appointments through the website?"

"Only a few. Which is why I'm upping my social media game. I'm going to target potential clients by connecting with first-time home buyers, young couples and single career folk."

"Sounds like a plan," Scarlet said, making her way to her desk. She had to get something similar in motion to sell the Perez house before Mr. Perez pulled it from her listings.

A framed photo of Scarlet and her mother greeted her as usual, pulling a more authentic smile across her lips. In the image, the Wills women stood arm in arm beside a SOLD sign and in front of a big white farmhouse. Scarlet had just gotten her real estate license and, under her mom's guidance and tutelage, sold her first property at above the asking price. It was a moment worthy of its ornate silver frame.

She briefly considered calling her mom to tell her about the strange situation she might be in, but Scarlet also hated to upset her without reason. Having a mom for a best friend was wonderful but complicated. She wanted to share everything with her, but occasionally the stories needed editing. And others just weren't Mom appropriate. She couldn't even properly gush about the handsome man she'd met today because of his ties to the potential stalker.

Austin's lean, lithe body flashed back into mind, his dark eyes on her, a wicked half grin on his lips. It was enough to make her want to clutch her pearls, if only she'd been wearing them.

"I bet he has killer abs," she whispered to herself, setting up her laptop for the day.

"Who?" Lydia appeared with her breakfast protein shake, brows arched high.

Scarlet's face heated.

"Oh. You're turning red." Lydia pulled up a chair and sat, crossing her legs and leaning forward. "This is going to be good. Please dish. I love abs."

Scarlet laughed. "I didn't mean to say that out loud."

"But you did. So, let's discuss."

"I met a guy this morning," she admitted reluctantly. "He was…really nice."

Actually, she realized, *this is the perfect setup to our cover story.*

Lydia took a long swig from her shaker and waited for more.

"His name is Austin Beaumont, and he might stop by the office later. If you're here I'll introduce you."

Lydia's jaw nearly unhinged. "No. Way."

Scarlet wrinkled her nose at the strange look of shock on the other woman's face. "You don't want to meet him?"

"Scarlet," she said flatly. "You enormous out-of-towner." The younger agent spun in a dramatic circle on her chair.

"You know I've been here for four years—"

"He's a Beaumont. Of course I want to meet him. The Beaumont brothers are a main component in every Marshal's Bluff woman under fifty's secret fantasy life. And if they're being honest, probably plenty of the men too. The brothers are all older than me, but I've grown up hearing all about them. They're practically legendary. My grandmama says their dad and his brothers were the same way. The one called Dean got engaged last summer and broke a bunch of hearts."

Seeing one of the PIs taken off the market certainly would be heartbreaking, but not the brother Lydia had mentioned. "I met Dean today too."

Lydia threw up her hands. "Absolutely unfair. You know, that family did a calendar once to raise money for a local farmer who was losing his land. The photographer volunteered her services, and they sold enough calendars to save the farm and hire a crew for harvest."

Also not surprising. But a real missed opportunity. Scarlet would've cheerfully bought three copies of that calendar. One for her office, another for home and one for her mama, who was over fifty, but no one with any amount of good sense would ever mention it.

"How exactly did you meet them before work?" Lydia pressed.

A very good question. Scarlet considered her words. "Austin approached me on the street downtown."

Lydia's eyes bulged. "He just walked right up to you?"

"Yeah." She cringed, recalling him approaching her SUV in traffic. "He startled me, so I threatened to pepper spray him and call the police."

Lydia roared with laughter.

"After we got that misunderstanding sorted, he asked to see me again."

"Wow. Some people have all the luck," Lydia said.

True, though Scarlet had never thought of herself as that person.

Her laptop finished booting up, and she navigated to her email. The number of messages in her inbox knocked her back to reality. "I guess I'd better get busy."

Lydia rose and returned her chair to the empty desk beside her. "Fine, but I'm jealous. Of the guy and the inbox. One day my email will be full," she said, striding to her work space. "Until then, it's time for me to launch the social media campaign of my life."

Scarlet opened the newest email from Mr. Perez, following up on their chat by phone the previous night. He wanted a detailed plan for reaching more potential buyers with information on his property, and something in writing about selling the listing, at his price, in the next two weeks.

She chose to be thankful this was an email and not another phone call.

From there, the correspondences got easier. Past clients planning another move. Referral clients looking for advice. A few showing requests from families and couples she was already working with to find their new home. And three newly accepted offers, which meant a string of phone calls to banks and title agencies after lunch.

By three o'clock, her inbox was looking manageable, and her stomach was filling with butterflies. Just a few more hours before Austin showed up at her office.

An incoming message drew her thoughts back to work. Another showing request sent through the website's online contact form. She opened the email with trepidation and breathed easier to see a woman's name instead of a man's. Better still, the prospective client wanted to see the Perez home. The day just kept getting better.

"Lydia?" Scarlet said, checking the time and responding quickly to the request. "I've got a showing at the Perez home in forty-five minutes. I'm going to head out there now so I can set up before the potential buyer arrives. I want to grab some cookies from the bakery and fresh flowers from the florist. I should be back by six, but if Austin beats me here, will you let him know I won't be long?"

Her coworker smiled. "I will gladly regale him with my many wondrous stories of working with Scarlet Wills."

"I think offering him a bottle of water and a seat will be enough," she said, moving a little more quickly. "But since you said that, I'll definitely be back by six."

Lydia laughed as Scarlet made her exit.

The lines at the florist and bakery were short, and the drive to the Perez home was rural, so she easily avoided traffic.

The home was situated on multiple acres and set back from the road by about two hundred feet. A curving black ribbon of asphalt wound through a lush green lawn and past numerous mature oaks to a turn-around driveway outside the large two-story estate. The annual lawn and landscaping maintenance budget alone was more than Scarlet would make on the sale, and her cut of the asking price was more than some folks made in a year. Motivation to sell was high for more reasons than the owner's persistence.

She climbed out of the car, her purse on one shoulder, cell phone, car keys and a bag with cookies in one hand. A bouquet of fresh-cut flowers rested in the crook of the opposite arm. She closed the door with a flick of one hip and took a moment to admire the estate.

It was nearing five o'clock, making this the perfect time for a showing. There was still enough daylight for a potential buyer to appreciate the exterior beauty on their way inside, and by the time they headed home, an array of auto-timed landscaping lights would illuminate the home and driveway, showcasing the equally brilliant curb appeal by night.

She took two steps before something in the air

seemed to change. The soft crack and grind of pebbles underfoot was her only indication she wasn't alone before an arm snaked around her middle and a gloved hand covered her mouth.

Scarlet's scream was squelched by the band of leather crushing her lips against her teeth. Air rushed from her lungs, pressed out by an unyielding grip across her center. The bag of cookies and fresh bouquet crashed to the ground at her feet. She jerked and kicked, fighting uselessly against an unseen attacker.

Hot, sticky breath blew across her temple and cheek. The scratch of his unshaven face scraped against her ear. "Stop fighting, Scarlet," he warned in a low, gravelly whisper. "I'm here to let you know I saw what you did this morning, and I won't tolerate you seeing him again." The rage behind the whisper stilled her limbs. "We can't be happy together if you won't be faithful. Understand?"

She nodded quickly, adapting as he changed the scenario. She'd expected to be dragged off somewhere and killed. Maybe there was hope after all. A warning meant a second chance. Didn't it?

That was all she needed.

"Good," he said, loosening his grip slightly. "Now, I'm sorry to do this, but you have to be punished. Otherwise you might forget we had this little talk or think you can try me again. You can't."

"No. No, no, no, no," she murmured against the glove. "I'm sorry. I'm sorry."

"Shh. This is going to hurt me more than it hurts you."

Scarlet's limbs tightened, and she braced for what would come next.

His hand left her mouth, and for one beat of her heart, she was free.

Then ten long angry fingers curved around her throat and squeezed.

Chapter Five

Austin wiped the back of one hand across his brow and adjusted the brim on his baseball cap to better block the sun. He'd scrambled to off-load as much of his work as possible over the past few hours, clearing his schedule to better focus on Scarlet's case. He now owed multiple favors to Dean, and had a mere hour from meeting with his gorgeous new client again, he was baling hay at the family ranch and hoping his other brother Lincoln would agree to one little thing. "So, you'll handle it?"

Lincoln made a noncommittal sound.

Austin stifled the urge to toss the next bale at his brother.

There wouldn't be time to go home and shower thanks to this delay. He'd have to show up at the Coulter Realty office looking and smelling like someone who'd just filled the bed of a pickup truck with hay. Twice. He was on a real roll with bad impressions today.

"Lincoln," Austin pressed. "Just tell me you'll do it, so I can meet with the new client."

His brother sighed. "You're calling this a reconnaissance to make it sound more appealing, but I'll actually be sitting in my truck alone all night staring at a dark house and trying to stay awake. I can't even drink coffee to pass the time, because then I'd need a restroom, and I can't leave."

"But it's easy money," Austin said. "And it pays in cash."

"I don't need cash."

Austin tugged the work gloves from his hands and frowned. He always forgot that about his brother. Being an officer in the military for several years, most of which he'd spent deployed, had paid him well. And without actual expenses, the money had piled up. Then, he'd come home to reinvent himself as a hermit, working full-time for the ranch. Considering his earn-to-spend ratio and general lifestyle choices, Lincoln wasn't money motivated.

He eyeballed his brother—tan and fit, bearded face and overgrown hair. The picture of a guy with nowhere to be and zero cares to give. Very few things interested him. One was solitude and the other was a blonde. "No one said you had to go alone. Take a friend."

Lincoln's jaw set, and his gaze swept over the stables, likely thinking of the young manager, Josie.

"And if you do this," Austin added, sweetening the pot before he said no. "I won't ask you for another favor for a month."

That raised one of Lincoln's eyebrows and snapped his attention back to Austin. "Six months."

"Two."

"Four."

Austin offered a bland expression. "I can say four, but we both know I'd be lying."

Lincoln rubbed a hand over the back of his neck. "Yeah, all right."

It wasn't abundantly clear if that was an acceptance of the offer or the fact that Austin would definitely need another favor in the next two months, not four, but he took it. "Thank you." Then he checked his watch again. "I might even have time to shower if I do it here instead of running home. And if I borrow some of your clothes."

Lincoln closed the tailgate and leaned against the old farm truck. "What's mine is yours, I guess." He scanned Austin, looking more interested than he had so far. "Do you think there's a real threat for this lady? Or do you just like her?"

"Both," he admitted. "She's beautiful. Successful. Smart. I looked her up online after she left the office. Based on her social media profiles, she doesn't seem to do a lot outside of work. Her personal posts are limited. The accounts for business are another story. I'm guessing that's how she attracted whoever's following her. I'd like to think she's being overly cautious, but if she's concerned enough to meet with a private investigator, there's almost always a problem."

"And you like her."

Austin looked over his shoulder toward their parents' home on instinct. "So far there's nothing not to like. Don't bring it up to Mama. I just met this woman.

She's going to be a client. Not an addition to the family."

Lincoln grinned. "That's not what Mama would say."

The sound of tires on gravel pulled their attention to an approaching truck. Their youngest brother, Finn, waved an arm through the open window.

Austin moved in the truck's direction, a sensation of unease rolling down his spine. "Were you expecting him?"

"Yeah." Lincoln kept pace at his side. "One of the new boarders was involved in some petty crimes. The ranch took responsibility for her until the trial. Finn's been around every day or so to check in."

Finn parked beside Austin, then met his brothers halfway across the lawn. "Didn't expect to see you here." He adjusted the dark sunglasses over his eyes. The shiny detective badge on his belt announced his authority, even if he looked far too young for the role.

"I was just here asking for favors," Austin said.

Lincoln grunted. "He pawned his current work onto me so he can meet with some cute new client."

Finn turned widened eyes on Austin. "How'd you manage that?"

"I'm not allowed to ask him for anything else for a month."

"Two," Lincoln corrected.

Finn laughed. "Solitude beats cash, huh?"

"Solitude is priceless."

"Tell me about the cute new client," Finn said, still grinning.

Austin rolled his eyes and explained the situation

with Scarlet Wills, then tipped his head toward the house. "I'm going to hit the shower here and try not to be too late reaching her office."

Finn looked up from his phone. He'd started scrolling the minute Austin had given Scarlet's name. "She's got a big web presence. Thousands of followers. If she's picked up a stalker, you're going to have your work cut out for you. She probably talks to a hundred people every week. Buyers, sellers, security companies, maintenance companies, landscapers, home stagers… Could be anyone."

"I'm aware." He'd already made lists to address categorically at their meeting tonight. "This is not my first rodeo," Austin reminded him.

Finn flipped up his palms in innocence. "You're right. You've got this. But let me know if you need an assist."

Austin took a few backward steps in the direction of the farmhouse. "Sounds good. I've got to get moving. I'm officially late."

"You're always late," his brothers called behind him.

They weren't wrong, but it was something he was working on.

Twenty minutes later, he'd showered and dressed in a new T-shirt and jeans from Lincoln's closet. Nice ones that Dean had purchased at Christmas, and Lincoln had promptly stashed in his closet without even removing the tags. Dean liked nice stuff. Lincoln found that entertaining.

Austin was glad for both truths, because now he

didn't have to dress in Lincoln's worn-out and holey favorites. He ran a hand through wet hair as he made his way onto the porch.

Finn nearly knocked him down on the steps, more focused on his phone than where he was going.

"Whoa!" Austin sidestepped, barely avoiding the collision. "Where's the fire?"

His brother's brows were gathered low when he lifted his gaze. "The Realtor you're meeting with—Scarlet Wills—"

The chill he'd felt earlier returned to Austin's skin. "Yeah?"

"She's at the ER. Come on. I'll drive."

Tension coiled through Austin's limbs, and he shot a hand out to catch his brother's elbow. "What happened?"

"Someone attacked her this afternoon. Stole her phone, purse and car keys. She managed to get into her car and start it before the key fob was out of range. She locked the doors and used her onboard system to call for help. She was unconscious when they arrived. She had your card in her hand."

Austin was in motion, truck keys in hand. "I'll follow you. Use your lights."

Finn kept pace, making a run for his truck.

Scarlet had been hurt while Austin had bantered with his brothers. And her attacker had taken everything he needed to find or reach her anywhere she went. Which meant Austin had severely dropped the ball.

That wouldn't happen again.

Chapter Six

Scarlet woke with the sunrise the next morning. She'd been admitted at the hospital for observation after being rescued, treated for her injuries and given a battery of tests. Her head, neck and shoulders screamed with each small movement, but she was glad for the daylight creeping across her windowsill. It'd been a long night of interruptions and drug-hazed nightmares.

Thankfully, aside from being unprecedentedly sore and permanently traumatized, she was more or less fine.

She blinked against the reaching shafts of amber and apricot light and turned to stare into the even brighter hallway. A groan escaped her lips and the sound elicited fresh pain from her tender throat. Memories of the attacker's hands around her neck came rushing back, along with the pungent scent of leather. The once-pleasant smell would forever haunt her now. Just one more way the jerk would continue to ruin things for her, even after she'd physically healed.

Other details about the previous night were fuzzy. She'd spent the wee hours waffling between attempts to fill in the blank spots and not wanting to remember at all. She'd been strangled. That part was crystal clear, and the rest didn't matter.

She hadn't seen the person who did it. Couldn't identify him by face or voice. Hadn't even gotten a look at what he drove when he made his escape.

There had been pain and fear. Struggle. Then blackness.

She'd climbed into her car and locked the doors, then pushed the starter button, not realizing her keys were no longer in her hand or pocket. The next thing she knew, she'd been on a gurney headed into the hospital. A padded collar around her neck. Straps holding her torso to a backboard. Blinding light everywhere.

Kind of like now.

Except everything smelled of bleach and…flowers?

She squinted at a pair of bouquets beside a pitcher of water and small plastic cup on her nightstand.

"I'm headed that way now," a female voice said.

Scarlet spotted a redheaded nurse moving toward her open door with a wide smile.

Several other women in matching scrubs were gathered outside her room, clutching clipboards and smiling goofily at something unseen.

The redhead stepped inside. "Oh, and it looks like she's awake. Good morning, Scarlet. How are you feeling?"

Scarlet's throat was tight and raw, so she did her best to look pleasant instead of speaking.

"Pardon me, ladies," a familiar tenor declared, seconds before Austin Beaumont strode into the room behind the nurse.

Scarlet's heart rate rose, and her muscles tightened. A million insecurities raced through her addled head. This wasn't the way she wanted to look when he saw her again. Or when anyone who didn't work as medical staff saw her at all. She was hurting and battered, sleep deprived and wearing a hospital gown.

She wanted to order him out. Or at least brush her hair, but her eyes chose to fill with tears of defeat instead.

Austin's right hand curled around a disposable cup. His opposite hand plunged deep into his pocket. The congenial expression he'd worn a moment prior vanished.

"Good morning," the nurse said, turning on a light over the machines and checking the monitors before facing Scarlet. "Your pulse is elevated. How's your pain?"

Scarlet cleared her throat, wincing immediately at the dull throb in her temple.

"Take these," the nurse said, passing her a pair of white pills. "We'll send a prescription home with you." She poured water from the pitcher into the plastic cup and waited while Scarlet took the pills.

"All right. Everything else here looks good. I'll catch the doctor and find out where your discharge stands."

Scarlet watched the nurse leave then slowly turned her eyes to Austin, wishing she was at least wearing her own pajamas, and that she'd been wrong about someone following her.

"I'm sorry," he said, taking a cautious step in her direction. "Scarlet. I'm so very sorry."

Her bottom lip trembled as his compassion pushed her toward the edge. "I didn't want to be right," she croaked. "Celebrities and social media stars get stalkers. Not small-town real estate agents. I just can't—" Her throat ached and words failed her, so she pleaded with her eyes. "I shouldn't have gone to that appointment alone."

"This is not your fault." He set his coffee on the stand beside her bed and gripped the metal rail near her arm. "You did everything right. You sensed something was wrong, and you sought help. I started building your case file and off-loading my work as soon as you left my office so I could concentrate on this. You had no reason to anticipate an attack."

Scarlet bit her lip, knowing that was true. She'd never in her wildest dreams thought she'd be brutally attacked like this. Followed again, maybe, but she'd asked for help with that. "What are you doing here so early? The sun's still rising. How'd you even hear about what happened?"

"My brother Finn is the detective on the case. He filled me in on as much as he can."

She worked the words over in her mind. "I hope he didn't wake you. There isn't much you can do here."

He shrugged. "It seemed smart to come as soon as I could. I feel better knowing you have someone keeping watch."

Scarlet's mouth went dry, and she sipped from her cup again. Did he believe her attacker was still watching? That he'd come to the hospital for her? The thought coiled her gut. "I know it's important to make a statement as soon as possible, before I forget the details, but it's all just—" she moved her hands in circles around her head "—scrambled. Or missing."

"Don't worry about that right now. Finn will check in when he can. Rest. Heal."

A soft rap against the door frame made her jump. Apparently she was more on edge than she'd realized.

The doctor who'd cared for her upon arrival gave a slight nod. His white lab coat had a photo ID clipped to the pocket. The words *Dr. Lanke* were embroidered on the opposite side. "You're up early," he said, moseying forward with a warm, parental smile.

Austin offered the older man his hand. "Austin Beaumont."

"Dr. Lanke." He looked curiously at the PI then swung his attention to Scarlet. "Would you like your friend to step outside while we go over your details?"

Scarlet glanced at Austin. She wasn't sure which details the doctor planned to share, but she also wasn't in a hurry to be without him. "It's okay. He can stay."

Dr. Lanke explained the results of some tests they'd been waiting on and recapped things she already knew. "Nothing broken or fractured. No signs of a concussion. Bruising and swelling around the throat will reduce on their own. Rest and hydrate. Take the pills for pain as prescribed so your body can relax and heal steadily without becoming overwrought. Follow up with a counselor within a few weeks, even if you think you don't need further help. Sometimes these things sneak up on us when we're sure we've gotten past them, and something like this should be talked about."

She nodded. "And my missing memories? When will they return?"

He took a breath, releasing it slowly and donning the fatherly smile once more. "The memories will likely return in time. It's not uncommon for patients who've been through trauma like this to suppress the specifics. The mind is a complicated thing, and it will go to great lengths to protect itself."

She slouched, defeated and deflated. It was bad enough that this had happened, but she'd reasoned that everything had a silver lining, or at least a purpose. For example, if she could remember the attacker's face, his car or some other detail that would lead the police to his arrest, then maybe it was worth the trauma, because this would finally be over. But she couldn't remember.

"I'll get the discharge paperwork together, and one of the nurses will bring it around shortly. Alternate ice for swelling and heat for comfort on your sore muscles. Be kind and patient with yourself. Change the bandage on your shoulder daily. I'll send a tube of cream for the stitches."

"Stitches?" she asked, taking a mental inventory. Her shoulder was sore, but so was the rest of her.

"You fell," Austin said, before the doctor could clarify. "Police found blood on a landscaping stone near the driveway's edge. The impact was enough to split the skin."

Dr. Lanke frowned but nodded. "We cleaned the wound and secured it with a couple of stitches to reduce scarring. Nothing serious, but it will be tender as it heals."

"Thank you," she whispered. The words left her lips absently while her mind struggled to imagine the scenario Austin described.

"Pretty flowers," Dr. Lanke said, tucking his clipboard beneath one bent arm. "From you?" His eyes flickered to Austin.

"Yes, sir," Austin said. "My partner and I. The others are from her coworkers."

Scarlet's heart thudded, and her stomach dropped. Did everyone in her immediate world know what had happened? The possibility nauseated her. She wished no one knew, but keeping a secret like this for long in a town as small as Marshal's Bluff would be impossible. Her attack had probably made front-page news.

She rubbed her palms against her arms, trying to scrub away the sensation of her attacker's hands on her skin.

"You're lucky to have such a dedicated fan," the doctor said. "Most boyfriends don't stay all night like this. Not that any of the nurses minded having him around." He chuckled and winked then headed for her door. "I'll get that discharge paperwork moving. You'll be free to go later this morning."

Scarlet's attention snapped to Austin and her lips parted. "You've been here all night?"

Austin looked sheepish. "I couldn't leave you again. I stayed in the waiting room so you could rest. I can't stop thinking this wouldn't have happened if I'd started shadowing you sooner, instead of putting it off until the end of the day. It's possible this happened because you came to see me. If my presence in your life escalated your stalker, then I wasn't there to protect you—" He shook his head, expression darkening.

She let his words roll around in her head, unable to properly focus on or dissect them. Something else was already pressing to the front of her addled mind. "You told the staff you're my new boyfriend?"

"They assumed," he said. "I didn't correct them. I know we hadn't decided on our cover story yet, but I needed a good reason to hang around. Couldn't let them think I might be a stalker." He frowned. "That was very unfortunate and poorly timed wording. Sorry."

Scarlet's lips curled into a small, unexpected smile. She was certain the nurses she'd seen earlier would let Austin do just about anything he wanted without question, but she kept that to herself.

"If I've overstepped, I'm happy to set the record straight with the staff."

"No." She shook her head. "It's okay. I implied as much to my coworker, so—"

"So," he echoed, lips twisting. "I guess it's official."

Her toes curled beneath the scratchy bleach-white blankets. It was definitely official. She was into her new protector in ways that would surely get her hurt in the aftermath. "Yep."

SOMETHING IN SCARLET'S eyes told Austin she liked the sound of them as a couple as much as he did. The fact that she could manage a blush after all she'd been through gave him hope for her full recovery as well. Physical and emotional.

He'd met his share of people who'd experienced terrible things. They all healed at their own pace. Some never spoke of their trauma again. Others addressed their pasts only as necessary. He suspected Scarlet was the type to form an awareness group, hold rallies and raze offenders like hers to the ground. He liked that about her. More than he should.

"I had a second reason for letting the staff believe we're dating," he admitted in the interest of full disclosure. "I can't be sure if your attacker saw you at my office, if he saw us talking on the street or sidewalk, or none of the above. But I don't want him to know you hired a PI. That knowledge could cause him to look more closely at the trail he's leaving while he follows you. We want to keep his focus on you, so Dean, Finn and the local police have the best chance of identifying and locating him quickly."

Scarlet swallowed audibly, and the pulse point in her neck beat faster. She sipped from her little cup again.

"I didn't say that to frighten you. I'm only being forthright." Austin leaned closer, expression firm. "I won't let him get near you again. You can believe that. He can't get past me, and he sure as hell can't go through me."

Her lips parted and her eyes widened as she watched

and listened, hopefully realizing every word was true. Austin was more than capable of bringing down any enemy, and she could bank on that.

Satisfied, he nodded and straightened.

"But you can't stay with me forever," she said. "What happens when you're gone?"

It was a solid concern, but clearly she didn't know him. "I won't leave until this guy's caught or you order me away. Even then, I'll probably still be outside in my truck." He did his best to refresh his smile and lighten the mood. But he'd meant those words too. Whoever had hurt Scarlet was going to pay for it, preferably by way of extensive jail time.

She cringed.

Maybe telling a woman, who was being actively stalked, that he too planned to follow and watch her indefinitely wasn't the encouragement he'd intended. "That sounded less creepy in my head."

Scarlet gave a small laugh, and her eyes fell shut. She opened them a moment later. "Well, the pain pills are kicking in." She raised a hand to her temple, then frowned as her fingers traced the goose egg at the side of her head.

He'd seen worse lumps on himself and all his brothers at one time or another, but it was different seeing the knot on her. The pain of her wounds seemed to form an anvil in his chest.

She lowered her hand to her lap and looked through the open doorway. "What happens after I'm discharged?"

He considered his words before speaking this time,

knowing whatever he said would be a shock on some level and wanting to ease that stress if he could. "I'll take you home, if you're comfortable with that. You shouldn't be driving or alone for a while. If you'd prefer someone else, I can call them for you. Or you can borrow my phone."

Her brows furrowed as she looked around the room. "I dropped my phone."

"We believe your attacker took it with him when he left."

She sank back against her pillows. "And my keys. I was in my car, but I remember being surprised when it started. I couldn't drive anyway. My vision was blurry. I was going to pass out."

He nodded, widening his stance for stability. The pain in her eyes might've knocked him back a step otherwise. "Paramedics broke your window when they arrived. You were unconscious. The police towed your vehicle, which is being treated as a crime scene now. Finn will have the window replaced when they finish. He'll let us know when it's ready, but that might be a few days."

"So I don't have a phone or car?"

"Not at the moment, but I can get you a phone," Austin said. He and Dean kept several at the office for situations like these. He might even have one in his go bag. "And I can be your chauffeur, assuming you don't mind riding in my truck. It's about ten years older than your SUV with none of the added comforts."

She wrapped her arms around her middle. "My

purse had my driver's license in it. He's got my home address. And a key to my house."

Austin dipped his chin in acknowledgment. "You won't be alone there, and I'm going to change your locks as soon as we arrive."

"Delivery," a perky female voice called from the doorway.

He turned as a young woman stepped into the room carrying a tall glass vase and two dozen long-stemmed red roses. Austin frowned. "That's quite a bouquet."

"Isn't it?" the woman said, making room for the huge arrangement beside the other, more appropriate-sized ones. "Someone must really love you."

Scarlet's gaze jumped to Austin as the woman took her leave.

"May I?" he asked, already reaching for the card. "Yes."

He plucked the small white rectangle from a thin plastic stake hidden among the baby's breath and greenery.

Two hastily scrawled words sent fire through his core.

I'm sorry.

Chapter Seven

Austin's focus jerked to Scarlet.

"They're from him, aren't they?" she asked, face pale and expression grim.

"I think so. I'm going to catch the woman who delivered these and find out. I won't be long."

She nodded, and he dove through the door.

"Excuse me," he called, too loud for hospital etiquette. A dozen nearby faces turned in his direction. "Wait," he instructed the woman who'd made the delivery.

Then he turned to the nearest nurse. "I need someone to guard Scarlet Wills's room until I get back. Don't let anyone in or out who isn't already assigned to her care."

The nurse nodded, eyes wide, then dashed toward Scarlet's room. Another nurse followed on her heels.

Austin jogged to the delivery woman's side, noticing the name Marie on her badge for the first time. He passed her the little card. "Did you take the order for these flowers?"

She stared in surprise and nodded. "Yes."

"Can you describe the man who wrote this?"

"I wrote that," she said. "I was in a hurry to complete the order and make my rounds." She motioned to a small rolling cart with an array of flowers, teddy bears and helium balloons. "I like to fill and deliver all the orders that came in after hours as soon as I get in each morning. He ordered the roses before I'd finished loading the cart."

Austin stilled. Marie had written the card. "Was the order placed online? Or did he come into the gift shop? Can you describe him?"

She shook her head. "He called."

"I need you to show me the receipt. Did he pay cash? Does the shop have caller ID?"

The woman looked skeptical, possibly borderline frightened.

"Please," he added, before she could make an excuse or do anything else that would cost him precious time. "I believe the person who sent those roses is the same person who attacked the woman in that room last night. I'm a private investigator, and I'm trying to find him." He pulled his credentials from his wallet as proof and waited while she looked at them. "Help me," he pleaded.

Marie grabbed her cart. "Okay. Let's go."

They hurried to the first-floor gift shop, where she passed her cart and delivery duties to a clerk behind the counter. She took the other woman's position and waved Austin to join her.

"Here." Marie pointed to the phone beside the register.

Blessedly, the device had caller ID.

Next she pulled the receipt tape from the register and matched the time of purchase to the time of the call. Another stroke of luck, likely thanks to the early hour. The phone only stored ten numbers, and his was still in the system.

Austin snapped a photo of the phone number before it was replaced by additional incoming calls. "I assume he paid by credit card. Do you remember the name on the card?"

She pressed her lips together. "It was a prepaid card."

Of course it was. Austin had to give the criminal credit. He was a planner and a thinker.

"May I have the number of the card?" he asked.

The woman frowned. "I think that's crossing some kind of line. I don't want to get fired."

"Can I ask your manager?"

"She comes in this afternoon."

Austin fought the urge to argue. Marie had her protocols too, and she'd already shown him more than she had to. "My brother is the detective on this case. I'll reach out to him. Maybe he can contact your manager."

She nodded. "Thank you. I'm sure that will work."

"Can you help me with one more thing?" he asked, pointing to the handset on the desk. "I'd like to call the suspect. He's more likely to answer if I use the gift shop's phone."

She glanced nervously around. "Okay."

Austin accessed the speaker function and dialed. He pressed one palm against the counter as he listened to the tinny rings.

"Hello?" a low and cautious male voice answered.

Marie's eyes bulged.

Austin motioned for her to talk then scratched a note on a flyer.

"Hi," she said, eyes scanning the paper. "This is Marie from the Marshal's Bluff Memorial Hospital Gift Shop. You placed an order for roses this morning, and I forgot to ask your name."

Austin nodded at her.

She'd done well.

The man's breathing became audible, and a rumbling laugh broke through the line. "Someone told you to call me. Didn't they?"

"No. I was just taking the flowers up and—"

"Don't lie!" he screamed.

Marie jumped back from the receiver, one hand pressed to her chest.

Austin set a palm on her shoulder. "Who is this?" he asked, raising the phone to his ear. "Tell me now, and I'll go easy on you. Make me work for it, and I'll be forced to remind you later that you blew this opportunity."

"Stay away from her," the voice warned. "Stay away. Or you'll regret it."

"I'm definitely not doing that," Austin answered, contrasting the other man's seething tone with a jovial one. "But I am coming for you." He smiled as he spoke, and Marie shot him a curious look.

Scarlet's stalker began to growl. The sound climbed into a wild scream. "She's mine! She's! Mine!"

A round of earsplitting cracks and booms made

Austin cringe. It sounded as if the man was beating his phone against something hard, possibly until it burst into pieces, because the line went dead.

"Oh, dear," Marie whispered, moving her trembling hand from her chest to her lips.

Austin dragged a nearby stool from its position in front of the register to within Marie's reach, and she sat. "Do you need me to call someone so you can take a minute to gather yourself?"

She shook her head.

He wasn't sure she was all right, so he kept an eye on her while he dialed Finn and delivered the rundown, then sent the photo of the number on the memory display.

"You should've let me make that call," Finn said. "We could've traced it from the precinct."

"He wouldn't have answered a call from the police station," Austin said. "I called from the gift shop so he'd think there was a question about his order."

"This is the number?" he asked. "In the photo?"

"Yeah." Though Austin was certain that particular phone had been destroyed. "You'll have to come down here and talk with the shop's manager to get the credit card number, but they have it."

"I'm already on my way," Finn said. "If I'm lucky, he paid for the prepaid card with something linked to his name, but I'm rarely lucky. Still, I'll be able to track the card to the store where it was purchased. The store should have a time-stamped receipt. Then I can check the security camera feed from that time to see who bought it."

"He might've bought the card online."

"Don't say stuff like that," Finn said. "You're going to jinx me."

"Okay, Detective." Austin rolled his eyes and waved goodbye to Marie, who was still shell-shocked behind the counter. "Thank you."

She nodded, eyes wide and skin pale.

He should probably send her flowers later for her help. Then again, the stalker might've ruined flowers for her. "I'm going back to Scarlet's room," he said, both to Marie and to Finn. "She's being released this morning, and I want to be there when she gets her instructions."

"Stay with her," Finn said. "I hate everything you've told me about this guy. I don't want you to leave her side again."

"Believe me," Austin said, breaking into a run for the nearest bank of elevators. "I'm not planning on it."

Chapter Eight

It was afternoon before Scarlet was finally discharged. She left in her dirty skirt, socks and underthings, plus a logoed T-shirt from the gift shop. Her top had bloodstains, and she couldn't bring herself to put it on.

The sun was high in the sky when a young man in scrubs wheeled her into the pickup area outside the hospital's sliding glass doors.

"Ready?" Austin asked, opening the passenger door of his truck and offering her his hand.

She didn't answer. She wasn't sure. Much as she wanted to leave the hospital, leaving made her feel vulnerable. She hadn't been hurt at the hospital. She'd been mended there. And going home with Austin meant a whole other set of problems. For starters, he was a perfect stranger, and while she didn't have any reasons not to trust him, she'd been through an ordeal. No one and nothing felt quite as safe as it had before.

In other, more mundane concerns, she didn't have the capacity to be a hostess, and she wasn't in the habit of having company. Her home was her private domain. She met with friends at restaurants or visited their place. Now, she was on the spot to hold herself together and be congenial when all she wanted to do was cry or scream or pack up and move to Timbuktu.

And she still needed to call her mother. She quickly pushed that thought aside.

"Scarlet?"

Her name on his tongue pulled her back to the moment.

Austin stood before her, hand outstretched. The hospital staffer who'd been pushing her wheelchair waited for her to get up so he could move on with his day.

"Sorry." She gingerly set her hand in Austin's and ignored the instant buzz of chemistry as he pulled her onto her feet with ease.

He held the door while she climbed into the truck's cab, then shut it when she was inside.

The interior smelled of earth and hay, warmth and sunshine. The soothing scent of his cologne seemed to underscore everything else.

She winced as she fastened her safety belt; every muscle in her neck, shoulders, back and torso felt tender, overstretched and bruised.

Austin climbed behind the wheel, donned a pair of dark sunglasses and shifted into Drive.

She studied the space around her. He hadn't been kidding about the age of his truck. It was old, a model she remembered from high school, but well maintained. A pair of handcuffs hung from his rearview mirror, and she became suddenly thankful he couldn't read her mind.

"Do you prefer a certain radio station or type of

music?" he asked, punching buttons as they turned away from the parking lot.

"I usually listen to audiobooks."

He pointed vents in her direction and turned on the cool air. "What kind of books?"

Heat rushed over her cheeks, and for the smallest moment, she considered dodging the question. Or lying. "Romance," she said finally, uninterested in bending truths. Even less interested in explaining her preferences. "I like books about families and happy endings." She turned her chin away and braced for the joke.

There was always a joke.

"Who are your favorite authors?"

She looked at him. "You know the names of romance authors?"

He shrugged. "A few. Mama is a huge fan. I try to keep up when she tells me about whatever she's reading. I know it's important to her, even if it's not my cup of tea."

"What's your cup of tea?" she asked, more curious about him than his mother's favorite authors.

He glanced at her, then away. "I read a little bit of everything."

"Such as?"

"Mostly nonfiction." He flexed his fingers on the steering wheel. Was he nervous to have the spotlight? "I like information. I don't even care what kind. Everything's fascinating if you give it a chance."

Scarlet waited, curiosity growing. "What have you read about most recently?"

"Cooking, gardening, fishing, aviation, unsolved crimes."

Scarlet smiled. The idea that Austin spent his free time reading was incredibly attractive. The fact that he read indiscriminately about everything from cooking to crime was even better. She wondered how many people knew that about him. And she liked the fact that she did.

"What?" he asked, noticing her stare.

"You're a nerd," she said. "You look like that, and you've still got a big inquisitive brain. I like it."

"You like how I look, or my big, beautiful brain?"

She laughed. Her throat ached in protest, but she couldn't squelch the smile. "I didn't call it beautiful."

"You called it big."

Another laugh broke free, and she grimaced at the pain.

She turned her eyes to the view outside her window, allowing herself a moment to recover while admiring the landscape. Slowly, the scenery morphed from busy downtown streets to quaint little neighborhoods, then to the sprawling countryside.

Within minutes, rolling hills of green grass stretched to the horizon, topped by a cloudless blue sky. Punctuated occasionally with a farmhouse, cattle or a big red barn. The sun was high and hot as it beat against the glass, combating the truck's comfortable AC.

It wasn't until Austin made the turn onto her road that she realized what was happening.

"How did you know where I live?" She hadn't

thought to give him her address, and her driver's license was with the stalker.

"Dean put it in the new client file," he said. "But I could've found you without it."

She swung her gaze to him, befuddled and having completely forgotten about the details his brother had asked for when she'd made the appointment. Those moments and that phone call felt like memories from years ago instead of yesterday morning. Even more worrisome was what Austin had meant by the second statement. "How?"

"For starters, you bought your house." He raised his brows and his gaze flicked to hers. "Anyone can visit the county auditor's website and enter your last name in a property search. If they don't know how to do that, they can look at your social media."

"My accounts are all set to private."

"Not your business account." He looked her way once more. "You post daily about available homes, your life as a Realtor, and advice for buyers and sellers. You take pictures of your home and lawn, advising sellers to do this or that to spruce up their properties before listing them on the market."

That was true, but she was careful. "I never give my address or photograph the home directly."

"No, but you showcase landscaping features and additions recommended for curb appeal. Your house number is visible on the mailbox in more than one photo. It's small, but people can use their cell phones to enlarge the image. And anyone familiar with the area knows there are only so many sparsely populated streets with inlet views."

Scarlet rocked slightly as he turned onto her driveway. "You can see the inlet in photos of my patio?"

"Yes." Austin cut the engine and climbed down.

She flipped mentally through an array of her most recent posts, realizing how much she'd unintentionally given away. Sometimes she even took photos of a book on her legs while she sat in the sun. Did her stalker imagine those images were meant for him?

The passenger door opened, and she started.

Austin reached for her hand and helped her onto her feet at his side.

The air between them was charged, and if she hadn't looked like someone recently attacked, wearing yesterday's clothes, she might've thought the tightening of his jaw was a sign of attraction.

She turned to face the house. "Shall we?"

He pulled a large black bag from behind her seat then shut the door and followed her. "After you."

A warm heady breeze wafted through her freshly mulched flower beds, overflowing with native blooms. She inhaled and released several slow breaths, working her pulse back to a more normal range.

"You have a beautiful home," he said. His voice traveled to her ears from a few steps behind her. Appreciation colored the tone.

"Thank you. I got lucky on this one. I helped an older couple find a condo near their grown children, and they offered me first dibs. I bought it before it ever went on the market." And since they'd purchased the place for a tenth of its current value, they were happy with the fair market price she could afford. "I think they liked knowing I planned to preserve it." Anyone else would likely have demolished the little home and built something infinitely grander in its place.

Scarlet loved it just as it was.

She climbed the porch steps and leaned against the doorjamb. "I don't have any keys."

Austin set his bag down and removed a credit card from his wallet. He slid the card into the crack between the door and wall then gave it a shimmy. A moment later, the knob turned, and he opened her door. "Like I said, I'm changing the locks."

Scarlet blinked. Her stomach pitched. "The knobs are original," she said on autopilot. Nearly everything was original. She'd made sure of it, because that had been important until yesterday.

He squinted down at her, big hands on trim hips. "I can drill a hole in the door and add a dead bolt, so we can keep the knobs. Or I can replace the knobs with something more modern and secure. This," he said, tipping his head toward the open door, "doesn't cut it anymore."

"I can order new knobs online," she said. "They'll preserve the aesthetic while offering better security, but delivery will take a few days."

He seemed to consider her words. "Let's place that order tonight."

She nodded then led him inside, flipping on light switches as she moved, hoping her attacker wasn't hiding somewhere in the shadows. Austin closed and locked the door behind them as her limbs began to tremble.

Austin's hand brushed her back. "I'm right here," he said. "You're safe."

Her knees locked, and she looked at her home through new eyes. "What if he's here?"

Austin guided her to the sofa in her living space. "I'll be right back. If you see or hear anything that makes you uncomfortable, just holler, and I'll be back in seconds."

She kneaded her hands as he moved out of sight, listening as his footsteps softened in her adjoining kitchen then went silent in her dining room. She imagined him moving in and out of her two first-floor bedrooms and along the hallway in between. The bathroom and sunroom doors creaked open and closed on the far side of her home.

The steps groaned as he climbed to the second floor.

A few moments later, he reappeared and took the seat at her side. "It's just us. Can I get you anything? Tea? Water?"

She shook her head. "It's my house. I should—"

"You should rest," he said, interrupting. "That's the doctor's orders. Meanwhile, I need to secure your windows and find another way to reinforce your doors until the new knobs arrive."

"It's petty, I know."

"It's not," he said. "This is your home. You've worked hard to make it exactly the way you want it, and this guy doesn't get to change anything more about your life than absolutely necessary for your safety. I can stay here until the new knobs and locks are installed. Longer if he isn't arrested before then. As long as that's okay with you."

Scarlet wiped a renegade tear as it swiveled over her cheek. "Thank you. I'm grateful for your help. I just wish I could do something to contribute. He was close enough to me to do all this—" she motioned to her neck and torso "—and I can't even give the police a description. It's infuriating."

"You've been through a lot. Your memories will likely return. Give it time. I'm sure something will trigger them. Until then, focus on healing." He pushed onto his feet. "Are you hungry? I can make or order something."

"You're supposed to be my guest."

He wrinkled his nose. "I kind of invited myself, and you were just released from the hospital. I'm basically your caretaker," he said. "And if I don't feed you, someone is sure to revoke my privileges."

She kicked off her shoes and stood. "Well, we can't have that." She swallowed a wave of emotion, ready to escape to her room for a proper breakdown.

Of course Austin noticed. "Do you want to talk about it?"

"No. I'm going to take a shower and change into something comfortable and clean." She planned to burn the skirt, socks and underthings in the firepit out back or stuff them into the garbage can at her next opportunity. Anything and everything that could remind her of her attack needed to go. She might even trade in her SUV when it was finished being a crime scene.

"I can make some tea and sandwiches when you're ready," he said. "Or soup if that will be easier for your throat."

Scarlet shook her head. "I think I'll start with a large glass of red wine and go from there." She didn't wait for his response. She couldn't. Instead, she turned on her heels and marched into her bathroom, where the shower would cover the sounds of her cries.

Chapter Nine

Austin gave himself a second tour of Scarlet's home while she showered. On this round, he took his time to thoroughly inspect every nook and cranny. Not just the places an intruder could hide, but anywhere someone could gain access to the house or install an unnoticed camera.

It'd been too easy to break in, and that fact had stuck with Austin. No one was hiding inside, but that didn't mean someone hadn't let themselves in, done something nefarious then left without a trace. The possibility Scarlet's stalker could've established a way to watch her from inside her home made his skin crawl.

Thankfully, he found no signs of intrusion or surveillance.

He did, however, see an intense attention to detail on Scarlet's part. Visible in the design of each room and the maintenance of the original floors, baseboards and crown molding. It was as if someone had refinished every inch of wood, tile and marble in the place. No wonder she'd cared about the front doorknob. Her home was a personalized work of art.

The decor choices were more feminine than any-place he'd ever lived, including the ranch, but he didn't object to any of it. It was like walking through a magazine spread. From the floral accents, to the soft color palette, the abundance of pillows, cozy throw blankets and art. It was a different side of Scarlet than he'd seen so far. The serious businesswoman he'd met at his office had shown no indication that she might also wallpaper a half bathroom in butterflies or sleep beneath a wildflower-print duvet. He added these things to the fact that she loved to read and preferred romance books, specifically ones with happy families.

Her small mudroom overlooked the rear patio and the inlet. A washer, dryer and shelf for folding stood before the window. A drying rack with a rainbow of lacy underthings hurried him along before his mind had time to formulate too many ideas.

He was there to protect her, not to want her. Not like that. Yet in two days' time, his ability to maintain professionalism was already being challenged, internally anyway. And that was before he'd essentially moved in with her.

He tried to imagine for the dozenth time how she'd managed to drag herself into her SUV and lock the doors before passing out. Or how she'd had the presence of mind to use her onboard system to call for help. She'd just been attacked. Strangled. Most people panicked in situations far less dire, but she'd maintained a level head and her quick responses might've saved her life.

Satisfied the home's windows and doors were secure, he went to make coffee and pour her wine.

She'd been gone awhile, but he imagined she needed extra time to process what had happened, to appreciate being home and to get through her usual shower routine when she was still so bruised and sore. She likely also needed a minute to adjust to the fact that there was a practical stranger in her kitchen making coffee.

Her bedroom door opened, and she emerged a few short minutes later.

Austin carried a glass of merlot in her direction, meeting her in the small hallway.

Her blond hair was darker, still damp from the shower. She'd piled it on her head and pinned it there. She smelled of shampoo and lotion, a delectable blend of uniquely Scarlet scents. Her cream-colored top clung to her athletic form. A pair of loose pink pajama pants covered her legs. "You remembered," she said, accepting the glass and taking a sip. "Thank you."

He smiled, enjoying the blush that spread across her cheeks and hating the angry red welts, now fully exposed, on her neck. "How are you feeling?"

"Better. It's good to be home with my things, in my space."

"And an uninvited houseguest?" he asked.

She offered a small, sad smile. "As long as he brings me wine, I won't complain much." She glanced down the hall toward her mudroom. "I'm going to sit on the deck. Do you want to join me?"

"I'll meet you there." He turned back to the kitchen

for a few things, including a fresh cup of coffee, then headed outside.

Scarlet's bras and panties were off the rack when he passed through the mudroom this time, tossed into a nearby basket instead.

He gave silent thanks for that mercy.

She looked up as he exited her home, wrapped in a soft-looking blanket. "I saved you a seat." She motioned to the white Adirondack chair beside hers; both faced the water.

"Thanks." He lowered onto the wooden seat and stretched his legs out before him. "I have something for you too."

"Oh?"

He lifted his cell phone into view. "I thought you might want to call someone. I still need to set up a phone for you, but you're welcome to use mine now. I'm sure there are plenty of people worried about you."

Scarlet stared at the device. "I think I'll wait. I'm not ready to talk about it."

"They're going to read about it in the paper."

She took another sip of wine. "I only care about my mother, and she doesn't live in Marshal's Bluff. I'll call her as soon as I can manage without crying."

Austin looked at her more carefully, noticing the puffiness around her eyes and slight redness of her nose. She'd been crying in the shower while he'd prowled her home. He should've—the thought stalled in his mind.

What could he have done? It was invasive enough that he'd come to her home and planned to stay. It wasn't as if he could've knocked on her door and offered her a hug.

"How's the wine?" he asked, pushing all thoughts of touching her from his mind.

"Exactly what I needed, though I probably shouldn't mix it with my pain pills."

He shrugged. The doctor had prescribed higher doses of the stuff readily available over the counter, nothing like a narcotic. "I'm sure a glass won't hurt."

"I doubt I'll even finish it," she said. "But a glass of wine on the deck has become symbolic to me. It's part of my routine, especially when I've had a hard day. It's peaceful out here. I swear some nights I can hear my tension rolling away in waves."

"The view is certainly beautiful." He looked away before she caught him watching her, fixing his eyes on the water instead.

"I don't always bring wine. Sometimes I have a cup of tea or a tall glass of ice water. It depends on the kind of day I've had. But the routine is tried and true."

Austin absorbed the autumn sun and salty breeze for several long moments, before moving on to his next gift. "I have something else for you."

She rolled her head against the backrest of her chair, an expression of relaxation on her features. "What?"

He shifted to pull the little weapon from his pocket and held it in the air between them.

She frowned. "What is it?"

"A compact stun gun. I thought you could practice using it a few times until you're comfortable, then keep it with you wherever you go. Especially until this is over."

"I have pepper spray and an air horn. And before you ask how well those worked for me yesterday, I want to point out that I wasn't able to get to them, and I wouldn't have been able to reach this thing either."

He bristled at her words, unhappy with whichever person in her life had made her think that would be anyone's response. "I wasn't going to say that."

She pursed her lips, eyes gliding cautiously over the device in his hand. "I'd probably just wind up shocking myself."

He also despised whoever had given her the idea there was anything she couldn't do right or well. "I'm sure that's not true."

She frowned, clearly unconvinced. "Can I think about it?"

"Absolutely. But just for fun, let me show you how simple it is." He hated pushing, especially now, when she'd finally found a moment of peace, but this seemed important enough to make an exception.

He held the small black cylindrical object on his palm.

"It looks like a flashlight."

"It does," he agreed. "And it even has a light, if you need it." He turned the device over until she could see one blunt end. "This little switch powers it on." He demonstrated. "This—" he pointed to a slider, flush with the side "—sets it to charge. And this—" he rested his thumb on a small red button "—stuns."

The device gave a menacing crackle, and Scarlet frowned.

"I have to be close enough to touch that little thing to the person's skin?" she asked.

He gave the device another look. He'd seen its small size as convenient. Looking through her eyes, it was easy to understand the problem. "I hope you'll never again be within arm's distance of someone who wants to cause you harm, but if that day comes, this will send them back a few steps and stop them long enough for you to get away."

He set the device on the small table at his side and turned his eyes to the inlet.

His peace was slowly slipping. He didn't like the thought she'd be alone if he wasn't there. She should be surrounded by friends and family while she pulled through this. If anyone in his family had been hospitalized, the waiting room would've been filled to capacity with folks hoping to wish them well. And a mile-long train of aunties bringing food would've wrapped the blocks outside their home. While her co-workers had sent flowers, the only person Scarlet had spoken of so far was her mama, and she hadn't even called her. "Are you and your mama close?"

She turned bright eyes to his. "Sure. She's my only real family and a great friend."

"And she doesn't live in town?"

Scarlet shook her head. "No. She lives in Holbrook. That's in the next county. Close enough to arrive quickly in an emergency, but far enough away to keep us from being competitors in the market."

He couldn't help wondering which part of the current situation she thought wasn't an emergency. "Have you considered visiting her for a few days while the police search for your stalker?"

"I have," she said. "I just haven't worked up the nerve to call and break her heart with this news."

Austin raised his coffee and returned his attention to the beautiful afternoon.

Wind rustled through her trees, jostling leaves in every shade from amber to crimson, and knocking a few handfuls loose. They fell like confetti against a backdrop of green grass and brilliant blue water. The view was enough to make him feel as if he was inside a painting. No wonder this was where she came to unwind.

"Do you think the police will find him?" she asked.

He didn't need to ask who she'd meant. And he was sure of his answer. "I do."

"And you'll stay with me until then?"

His heart softened with her wobbling words. He couldn't explain it logically, but he knew he'd stay with her as long as she needed. "I will."

"What if it takes a year? Or ten? You can't just give up your life and all your other clients. What will I do then?"

"Let me worry about my life and my clients. You have enough to think about. Besides, it won't take a year to find him."

Scarlet turned, fixing him with the full intensity of her ethereal green eyes. "How can you be sure?"

Austin leaned in her direction, matching the weight

of her stare. "Because whoever hurt you doesn't stand a chance against my family."

SCARLET WOKE THE next morning at nine. She hadn't slept past six in years, and it felt incredible, until she moved. Her aching body protested as she angled upward in bed.

A glass of water and a note sat on her nightstand, along with the painkillers the doctor had prescribed. The note had simple instructions a la *Through the Looking Glass*. "Eat me. Drink me," she read, smiling at the reminder that Austin Beaumont was running loose in her home.

She took the pills and headed to her bathroom to prepare for her day.

Memories of the previous night flashed in her mind as she combed her hair and brushed her teeth. Sitting with Austin on her deck until the sun had set. Watching movies with him in her living room while sharing snacks on the couch and talking about anything and everything to pass the time. She'd gotten to know him better in a few hours than she knew some of the folks who'd been in her life for years. And she hadn't learned anything she didn't approve of or admire.

He loved his family, all ten million of them. He was also smart, funny and kind. She'd felt safe in his care before, but now, she was looking forward to more nights like the last one.

She swiped her favorite tinted gloss across her lips and gave her lashes two coats of mascara before spending an extra few minutes on her hair. Soft jeans with frayed edges, fuzzy socks and a T-shirt from her office softball league completed the casual look. With any luck, he wouldn't realize how much she hoped he thought she was pretty.

Outside her bedroom, the house was quiet, save for movement in the kitchen.

"Good morning," she called, inching slowly in that direction. Hoping it was Austin and not her attacker shuffling around. "Hello?" she projected her voice as she drew nearer.

The scrape of a chair over tiles met her ears a moment before Austin said, "I have to call you back."

She exhaled in relief and pasted on a smile.

"Hey," Austin said, removing earbuds and rising from her table, where a laptop sat beside a pad of paper and a pen. The enticing scents of coffee and cologne filled the little room. "I hope you don't mind. I helped myself to the shower and your kitchen." He motioned to the pot of fresh brew on her counter. "Can I get you a cup?"

"Please."

"Cream or sugar?"

"Both."

He smiled. His outfit was similar to her own—faded jeans and a T-shirt with his PI company's name on the front. "This was all I had in my go bag," he said, following her gaze to his ensemble. "I borrowed something from my brother yesterday, which left this for today. We should probably visit my place soon for a few staples."

"Sounds good," she said, enthralled by the idea of

seeing Austin's home. What did it look like? What secrets would it reveal? The thrill of curiosity thinned when she realized he might live like a frat kid, eating out of pizza boxes and sleeping on sheets he hadn't laundered since moving in.

He passed her a steaming mug.

"Thanks." She inhaled the delectable aroma and exhaled a pound of distress. "I can make breakfast since you made the coffee. As soon as I get to the bottom of this cup and am officially awake."

Austin's gaze flickered to the clock on the wall then back to her. "I hoped to tell you sooner, but I've got breakfast covered."

"What do you mean?" She scanned the kitchen for an indication he'd prepared something already.

The doorbell rang.

"That's for me," he said, tipping his head to indicate she should follow. "Us, actually."

"You ordered breakfast?" She hurried along behind, shamelessly enjoying his use of the word *us*.

"Not exactly."

He opened the door and stepped back so she could move into the space at his side.

A middle-aged woman with a wide smile and milkmaid braids stood on the porch, a casserole in her hands and an insulated bag hooked over her wrist. "Good morning!" she said, big brown eyes swinging from Scarlet to Austin. "Hello, sweet baby boy."

Chapter Ten

"Morning, Mama." Austin stepped forward to kiss his mother's cheek before making room for her to come inside. "Scarlet just woke, and I haven't had time to warn her about your arrival."

She pinched his cheek. "Warn her? I'm here to help. Now, where's the kitchen?"

Scarlet blinked as the woman moved past, following her son to the stove.

"Scarlet," he said with an apologetic grin. "That's my mama. Mary Beaumont."

They followed on the older woman's heels. "Mama, this is Scarlet Wills."

"It's lovely to meet you," she said, setting the temperature on Scarlet's oven. "This just needs to be warmed a little. I hurried to get here so you wouldn't have to wait long."

"Thank you," Scarlet said, half amused, half in shock.

Austin's mom made casseroles and dropped what she was doing to race them to his clients? Scarlet's mom never cooked, barely ate and only rushed to get to business appointments.

"I made your favorite," Mary said, speaking to her son. "Fajita breakfast casserole. I brought all the fixings and some things for lunch and dinner. Snacks too. But y'all can come to the ranch for dinner if you'd like. It must be dull staying here around the clock. It might be good to get out."

"Said the spider to the fly," Austin muttered, causing his mama's smile to widen.

Scarlet watched them, mesmerized at the ease of their interactions and the way they moved in practically choreographed steps around the room. Putting things into her refrigerator, sliding the dish into the oven, setting the table for three. Clearly Austin had familiarized himself with her small kitchen while she'd slept.

Mrs. Beaumont made small talk as they worked, complimenting Scarlet's home and asking how she felt. She asked about her mother too and if Austin was being a good houseguest.

The initial shock of her presence was gone in minutes, and Scarlet was unprecedentedly at ease with another stranger. Like with Austin, Scarlet suddenly felt as if she'd known the older woman forever. And she laughed when Mrs. Beaumont told stories about life on the ranch raising five boys.

"And that's how this one got a scar above his eye," she said, poking Austin on the forehead. "He likes to say he fell from a bull, but that wasn't the story I heard."

Austin leaned away with a grin. "Dean said a blanket would work like a parachute if I jumped off the barn. He was fifteen, and I was ten. I thought he knew everything."

"Brothers," she said, pride evident in her eyes. "Do you have any siblings, Scarlet?"

"No, ma'am."

Mary reached across the small table and covered Scarlet's hand with hers. She searched her face a moment then said, "I know things probably seem pretty scary right now, but I promise you, my boys are working hard to change that, and they never fail."

She grinned, thinking of Austin's comment on her deck last night. "So I've heard."

"It's true," Mary said. "They're all very good at what they do, and they always get their man. Or woman." She winked.

"Mama," Austin warned. "Don't."

"What?" she asked, raising her shoulders to her ears. "I'm just offering her a little comfort. My boys never get involved unless they know it's worth the trouble, and they give 110 percent when it is."

Scarlet couldn't help wondering if Mary was still talking about finding a stalker, or if she'd moved on to something else.

"Did Austin tell you Dean just got engaged?" she asked. "I can't wait for the wedding. And the grandbabies. Do you want children, Scarlet?"

Scarlet's gaze jumped to Austin, who dropped his forehead into one waiting palm. "Yes?"

"Excellent," Mary said. "I know it's every couple's

choice, but I like to imagine the ranch filled with children one day when my husband and I are too old to keep all the teenagers. Then it will just be us, our children and our grandbabies."

Austin straightened with a laugh. "Mama would like to see my brothers and I populate a small town."

Mary beamed. "There's nothing wrong with wanting a big family."

"I always wanted five children," Scarlet said, unsure why the secret, silly fantasy slipped out.

"Really?" Austin and his mom asked in unison.

"Yeah." Scarlet laughed. "I don't know why five, exactly. Maybe it was a result of being a lonely only child, but I decided a long time ago five was the perfect number. Unfortunately, at twenty-seven and single, five is probably not in the cards these days."

"Well," Mary said. "You never know, do you? Twins are a possibility. So is adoption and being pregnant a lot." She laughed.

Austin looked horrified. "Mama."

"We're just having a little girl talk," she said. "I suppose you'd prefer to talk shop."

He looked as if he'd prefer to talk about anything else, and Scarlet regretted her candor. It wasn't as if she'd included him in her fictional family of seven. Still, he looked paler than she'd ever seen him, and it felt like she was the cause.

"Have you given her a Taser?" Mary asked.

"I tried," he said. "I offered a stun gun, but she wouldn't take it."

Her thin brows furrowed. "How about a pistol?"

Scarlet laughed. "No, thank you. I think I'd sooner carry the Taser."

Mary smiled. "Then it's settled."

The apple really didn't fall far.

The oven dinged, and Mary popped to her feet. "Time to eat."

"She loves us with food," Austin said.

"I'd never say no to that." Scarlet smiled. She'd only known Mary Beaumont a few minutes, but it was evident she loved her family in every possible way.

Scents of roasted red peppers, eggs, onions and cheese floated through the room, and her stomach groaned in anticipation.

"Eat up," Mary said, setting the casserole on the table between them. "Because I think the next thing we should talk about is how soon you can relocate."

"We're going to my place later," Austin said. "I need to pick up some things if I'm going to stay here, but you can always see what you think while we're there." He looked to Scarlet, avoiding his mama's knowing eyes. "It might be the better choice."

AUSTIN KNEW THE moment he suggested his place as a possible location for Scarlet's respite, his mama would latch onto it. But the words had practically leaped from his mouth the moment she'd mentioned relocation, which was an idea he wouldn't argue with. And he couldn't backpedal now.

His mama hitched a brow.

Everyone who knew the Beaumont family assumed it was their father, a former police chief, who inspired the boys to get involved in law enforcement or investigation. But anyone who'd spent any amount of time at the ranch knew Mama as the best detective among them. She saw, heard and sensed everything. The only time he or his brothers got away with something as kids and teens was when she'd decided to ignore it. Even then, she let them know she hadn't missed their transgression. Usually by doubling their chores for a week or two without comment.

Scarlet raised her mug, looking pleasantly calm on the outside, but her hand trembled as the drink reached her lips.

He didn't want to take her away from her home, and he'd been thinking of how to avoid it, but his mama was right. Scarlet's place wasn't the safest option. Changing the locks would help, but it would be days before the new ones arrived. Until then, the problem was sleep, or the lack of it. He couldn't remain perpetually awake and on the move for days, making his rounds from the front to back door all through the nights.

"Has Austin told you about our ranch?" Mama asked. "It's beautiful. Peaceful. There's always plenty of good food and even better people. There are animals too. A stable with horses if you like to ride. And you'd be safe. If you'd prefer someplace like that."

Scarlet returned her cup to the saucer with a soft clatter. "I'd like to stay here, if that's possible."

Mama tipped her head. "Anything's possible, but is it safe?" She looked to Austin. "How long before the door locks are changed?"

"By the end of the week," Scarlet answered. "I placed the order last night."

"And who will keep watch at your front and back doors until then?"

Austin fought a smile. He and his brothers had a running theory she was a mind reader. Times like these seemed to support that.

Scarlet's eyes darted to him. "How did you watch both doors?"

"I was on the move most of the night."

"You didn't sleep," she said flatly, and he could practically see the reality of the situation sinking in. The set of her mouth turned grim. "I slept better than I have in a long while."

Silence stretched around them.

Scarlet sat taller and turned to his mama. "I wouldn't want to risk bringing my danger to your ranch and the folks you're helping there. I hear you do wonderful things for young people with troubles of their own. I don't want to see this spread to anyone else."

His mama's gaze roamed Scarlet's features, and Austin wondered if she saw the things he did. Scarlet was brave and selfless. She'd been through hell, but still worried more about potentially exposing strangers to her attacker than about the added protection the ranch could offer her. "That's why you don't want to stay with your mama."

"Yes, ma'am."

"Hotels aren't ideal," Mama said, dusting her lips with a napkin. "They can be hard to guard properly if they're breached. But if you can check in unnoticed, under a false name, you might not be found. If you decide not to stay with Austin. There will be an added expense of course. And he'd still need to be there. At least with adjoining rooms."

Scarlet nodded, accepting his mama's input, which had obviously been worded to sway her against the notion.

Austin rested his clasped hands on the table, drawing both sets of eyes. "I can talk to my brothers about setting up shifts to keep watch here for a few days. Staying won't be a problem if that's what you want to do."

Scarlet frowned. "I hate to put out anyone else. You're all doing so much already. And if they're here all night, they'll be exhausted all day. That will only diminish their ability to search for whoever did this to me." She sighed. "That's counterproductive."

He dipped his chin once in agreement. "My place is still an option. It's not listed on the auditor's website as owned by me. Very few people know where I live. Dean and I went to great lengths to hide our addresses when we opened the PI business. I keep a top-notch security system, and I'm an excellent shot."

He bit the insides of his cheeks, regretting the comment about shooting trespassers, even if he had been joking. A little.

Scarlet snorted a small laugh, and his mother's smile widened at the poorly timed words.

"Well." Mama stood. "I should be getting back to help your father. Let me know what you decide and if there's anything you need. I've put a cowboy casserole in the freezer for dinner. Just take it out while the oven preheats, then pop it in for about half an hour, and it'll be ready to eat."

"Thank you," Scarlet said, rising to walk her to the door. "For everything. It was really nice to meet you, and your offer for me to stay at the ranch was very generous. I can see where Austin gets his kindness."

Mama's eyes flashed with pride, and she fixed him with a look over Scarlet's shoulder that could only be interpreted as immense approval.

He was sure to hear about it later.

Chapter Eleven

Austin and Scarlet waved from the porch as Mama drove away, and the moment felt so oddly natural, he wondered if his lack of sleep had pushed him toward delirium.

Scarlet turned on her toes, teeth pressed into her bottom lip and looking strangely excited. "I have an idea."

He frowned. "About?"

She shifted, averting her gaze before seeming to steel her resolve. "There's something I think we should do. You gave me the idea last night when you were encouraging me to relax and not worry."

His lips parted and all sensible thoughts left his brain. "What did I say?"

"That something would eventually trigger my memories, and they'd come back."

He fought a smile. He hadn't been sure what he'd unintentionally motivated her to do when this conversation started, but recovering her memories wasn't even on his radar. "What's your idea?"

"I want to go back to the place where I was attacked. Maybe being there will jar something loose."

She pretended to knock on her forehead. "What do you think?"

Austin grimaced, uncomfortable for all new reasons. "Are you sure about that? It hasn't even been forty-eight hours. There's no need to rush. I think your memories will return on their own, if you're patient. Your doctor told you to rest."

"Maybe I don't want to rest." She crossed her arms and squared her shoulders. "It's not as if I'm asking to run a marathon." She winced. "That sounded angry, but it wasn't directed at you. I'm mad because I can't remember anything about this guy. Meanwhile, he's out there running free, doing whatever he wants, when he wants, and my life is a wreck. I'm hurt. I've got a live-in bodyguard. I might have to leave my home. I can't go to work. And I hate that I can't be more helpful to you and your brothers when everyone else is doing so much for me."

Austin stepped closer, leaving only a foot of space between them, unsure if she needed a hug, or if he did. He'd already assured her, multiple times, that she didn't owe anyone anything for their help. "Returning to the scene of your attack will likely be traumatic. Your mind hid what it did to protect you, and going back might feel a lot like unloading a dump truck of stress onto your brain."

"Or it might not."

Austin crossed his arms, matching her stance. He wouldn't willingly cause her distress. But he wasn't sure he could deny her either.

"You said you were here to help." Her expression softened and so did her voice. "I think this will help."

Austin sighed. She was right. Her happiness outweighed his concerns, and he was in way over his head.

AN HOUR LATER, Scarlet was finally moving toward the front door.

She'd dragged her feet a bit while getting ready to leave. Mostly second-guessing herself, battling nerves and putting off the trip she'd suggested.

She stuffed her feet into brown suede booties and pulled her wool peacoat from the hook near her door. "Ready?"

"Yep."

She spun in the direction of his voice, hating the joy and comfort it brought when they'd only known one another a short time.

He stopped before her, having added a leather jacket and baseball cap to his ensemble. "I forgot to give this to you earlier," he said, reaching into his pocket. "You'd only been awake a short time before Mama arrived. By the time she left, you wanted to head out. Time got away from me." He passed her a cell phone.

She accepted the device, searching his eyes for more information.

"It's a new disposable," he said. "I had one in my bag like I thought. I opened it last night and set it up. I added myself, Dean, Finn and Mama to your contacts. Now you can call your mom when you're ready. Or a friend. Whoever you want."

A knot of unexpected emotion clogged her throat.

It'd been her experience that most people said lots of things they didn't mean. But every time Austin made a promise, he followed through as if it was the most normal behavior in the world. He probably had no idea how much little things like reliability and truth meant to someone who'd been played, scammed and generally run around by men since the moment she'd started dating. "Thank you."

She gave herself an internal kick for her constantly increasing interest in him. He was here because she'd hired him. Not because he wanted to spend the rest of his life in her arms, watching sunsets from the deck, raising children who'd never doubt how much they were loved.

The sound of keys pulled her out of the fantasy, and she followed Austin across the porch toward the driveway.

They were on the road, closing the distance between her home and the scene of her attack, in minutes.

She stared at the phone in her hands, trying not to think too hard about their destination. It had been her idea after all, and it was far too late to chicken out now.

"Thinking of calling your mama?" Austin asked.

"Yes, but I might call the office first. Lydia sent flowers to the hospital, and I never thanked her." She dialed without letting herself overthink the decision. Whether she wanted to talk about what had happened or not, Lydia deserved to know she was safe and healing.

"Coulter Realty," Lydia answered on the first ring.

"Hey." Scarlet's throat tightened, and she had to clear it before going on. "It's me."

"Scarlet!" Lydia gasped. "Oh, thank goodness! I've been worried sick. I almost drove to your house this morning when I didn't hear from you. I stopped at the hospital after work, and they said you'd already been discharged."

"I'm home and doing well," she said. "The flowers were pretty and very appreciated. I'm sorry I didn't call you sooner."

"The morning paper said you were robbed. How are you doing? Do you need anything?"

Scarlet cringed, having forgotten to worry about what the paper said, and hating that Lydia's voice was laced with pity. "I'm fine. I didn't see the paper."

Austin glanced her way.

"The article was awful," Lydia said. "I cried reading it. I can't believe something like that could happen here, and to someone like you."

Scarlet wasn't sure what her friend had meant by the last part, but her eyes misted with unshed tears anyway. "I'm okay," she croaked. "Or I will be. I'm with Austin, and he's taking good care of me."

Lydia made a wild sound in the back of her throat then squealed. "Oh, now I am definitely coming to visit you."

Scarlet slid her eyes in Austin's direction. The slight upturn of his lips suggested he'd heard the squeal, if not Lydia's very loud words. "Don't do that just yet," she said. "We might stay at his place for a few days.

The person who attacked me has my purse, so we know he has my address."

Lydia gasped again.

Had she always been so dramatic, or had Scarlet been emotionally numbed by recent events?

"Which reminds me," Scarlet added, pressing on. "I sent an email to the home office last night letting human resources know I wouldn't be in for the rest of the week. I can't exactly sell houses looking like I do." The knot at the side of her head seemed to throb on cue, and her fingers trailed up to touch the bruising around her neck. "I've reached out to all my appointments and asked if they'd like to reschedule. I've given your email to everyone who wasn't interested in waiting. I thought that was best. You can do the showings. Make the sales. Build your client list. And I won't look like a flake for canceling last minute. I hope that's okay."

"Are you sure?" Lydia asked.

"Absolutely. You're a fantastic agent, and I know they'll be in good hands. Call me back at this number if you need anything."

"Thank you."

Scarlet smiled. "Don't mention it."

She disconnected the call and refocused on the view outside. Her stomach tightened as Austin turned off the main road and onto Mr. Perez's driveway.

It was time to find her memories.

Chapter Twelve

Scarlet dropped the phone into the truck's cup holder, a rush of foreboding crashing over her as she stared through the windshield.

Austin cut the engine but didn't make a move to get out. Probably waiting for her to decide if she was sure she wanted to do this.

The Perez home was beautiful as always, a handsome estate on a gorgeous plot of land.

She was safe. She wasn't alone, and what had happened once at this location wouldn't happen again.

She repeated the ideas silently until they felt more like truth, then she reached for her door handle. "Okay. I'm ready."

"I brought the stun gun," Austin said. "In case you want to carry it for peace of mind or try powering it up while we're here."

She shook her head, releasing a slow breath. "One thing at a time."

Austin followed her lead when she opened her door and climbed out. Then he hung back while she moved to the driver's side.

Sunlight glinted off pebbles of broken glass on the driveway.

"They had to break your window to get to you," Austin said.

She nodded, feeling his eyes on her as she walked along his truck, pretending it was her SUV. Her limbs began to tremble and her breaths quickened, but her mind went numb.

She scanned everything in sight, willing the blank spots in her memory to be revived.

"You doing okay?" Austin asked.

Scarlet clenched her teeth. "Everything looks different," she said, trying out reasons her stubborn brain refused to cooperate. "It's earlier in the day. My SUV isn't here. I know this is where it happened, but nothing feels the same."

"That's good," Austin said, stepping nearer and setting a gentle palm on her arm.

Scarlet turned to glare. "How can you say that? This place was supposed to give me answers."

"It's good because you're not losing your mind right now. Some people can't ever return to the places where things like this happened to them. Even seeing similar scenes in a movie can be enough to trigger their fear and panic. I'm saying I'm glad you're doing okay right now."

She considered his words, and the soft pressure of his palm against the fabric of her coat. "Yeah, well, I'm on a mission, and I'd hoped this would be easier."

He pulled his hand away and wiped it across his

mouth, possibly fighting a grin. "All right. What's next?"

She wet her lips, making the procedure up as she went along. If being there wasn't enough, maybe the gruesome details would help. "Tell me what the police said," she suggested. "Maybe that will get the mental imagery going."

Austin looked skyward a moment, as if gathering his thoughts. "Finn said he spent about an hour out here walking the space, then circling the area in his car. There wasn't a lot to go on. He found some tire tracks in the grass along the road's edge, tucked behind that cluster of trees."

She followed his gaze and pointed finger to a dense cluster of pines. "I didn't come from that direction. I wouldn't have seen beyond the trees."

Austin nodded. "Your stalker probably knew that."

"He's smart," she said, wishing it wasn't true. "Like a conniving little fox."

"Pretty much. All the more reason to carry a stun gun."

She rolled her eyes. "You're persistent."

"I am," he said, releasing the mischievous grin she loved. The one sure to do her in if the unnamed stalker didn't.

Then another idea came to mind.

"I don't like that look," he said.

"What look?"

He stepped back. "The last time you made that face, you asked me to bring you here, and you wouldn't take no for an answer."

"Sometimes I can be persistent too," she said. "Especially when I'm right about something, which is most of the time. Like now." She twisted at her waist, scanning the area. "You won't like it, but I want you to humor me."

The apprehension on his face was nearly comical. As if she'd asked him to kindly remove his fingers. "Can you be more specific?"

"I want you to grab me from behind."

His eyes widened and his brows rose. "What?"

"Like an attacker," she clarified. "I think that could help."

"That is definitely not a good idea," he said. "For a whole host of reasons, I'm going to decline."

"You can't."

"I can." He took another step back. "I won't pretend to attack you. I don't want to upset you or put that terrible idea in your head, even if you think you want it. You don't."

"I decide what I want," she said. "Now, stop backing up. That's where I was standing when it happened."

Austin's gaze fell to the broken glass at his feet.

"I'd just gotten out of my SUV. I'd barely taken two steps before his hands were on me. He dragged me back to where I'd started. I thought he was going to take me to a secondary location and murder me."

Austin paled as she marched forward then turned in front of him, putting her back to his chest.

"Scarlet," he warned.

She shivered at the sound of her name on his lips and the feel of his breath against her hair. "Hush, please." She reached back and caught his wrists then pulled them forward. "One arm came around me here." She curved his arm around her rib cage. "The other covered my mouth." She guided his fingers to her lips, but he tensed, refusing to actually touch her. "Put your face against mine. On the right."

Two long beats passed before he did as she'd asked. His skin was warm and smooth as it brushed against hers, and her heart rate quickened.

"I don't like this," he complained.

"Shh." She closed her eyes and imagined the scene, allowing the fear to build inside her. "I think he had a beard or hadn't shaved." Her breaths grew shallow as she chased the memories. "I felt stubble on my cheek."

"Good," he said, attempting to lower his arms. "That's something."

"Wait!" She caught his wrists and jerked them back into place, momentarily crashing one arm against her tender torso and the fingers of his other hand against her mouth.

Austin cussed and sprang back.

Scarlet's eyes flashed open, catching his reflection in the truck's side-view mirror. But it wasn't Austin she saw there.

He looked horrified when she spun to face him, hot tears on her wind-chilled cheeks.

"I saw him in the SUV's mirror. He was tall, but shorter than you, and he had a beard," she said, the words pouring out faster than she could sort them. "He wore a dark gray hoodie. The hood was up, pulled over his hair. I don't know what color it was, and his eyes were cut off in the image."

Joy and adrenaline flooded her system, and she bumped the toes of her boots against his. "His shoulders were narrower than yours. His arms were thinner. I didn't know him. Or he didn't seem familiar."

Austin's hands rose to grip her elbows as a tremor rocked through her. "Breathe, Scarlet. This is all good, but you have to breathe. Do you want to sit?"

She shook her head, tears coming heavily as relief mixed with residual terror. "I did it."

"Yeah, you did." Austin pulled her against him, engulfing her in his embrace and resting his cheek against the top of her head. "You were fearless. And you're safe now. Okay?"

She nodded, tears soaking the thin cotton of his shirt. Her arms wrapped around him, beneath the unzipped bomber jacket. And another memory returned. "I think he wore leather gloves." A small, unexpected sob broke on her lips.

"It's okay," he whispered. "Just breathe."

Austin curved his body around hers, holding her close and feeling his protective instincts surge. She'd been through so much, and she'd willfully returned to this place, hoping to make a difference, even knowing the experience could break her. That was a whole other level of bravery. And he admired her for it. He'd seen soldiers behave similarly during his time in the military, and the mental connection was jarring. Scarlet was a civilian, but she was fighting her own war, where the enemy was violent and invisible. And she was alone in her experience, but still, she persisted.

He stepped back, dropping his arms to his sides, stunned by the turn his thoughts continued to take. He was too taken by her, and he didn't like the way it left him unsettled.

"Sorry," she said, looking embarrassed. "I didn't mean to—" She motioned between them.

"No. You're fine. I just—"

They stared at one another, tension twisting in the air.

"What would you like to do now?" he asked, hoping to appear more calm and centered than he felt. "We can swing by my place to get some things, or your office if you have anything you need to do."

"Can we go to the police station?" she asked. "Maybe I can tell Detective Beaumont what I remembered."

"Finn," Austin said, raking a hand through his hair. "Yeah. That sounds good. I'll call and let him know we're on the way."

They climbed back into his truck, and the air seemed thicker as he reversed down the driveway. He hadn't intended to hold her. Hadn't expected her to hug him. But she had, and he did, and now he knew what her heart felt like beating against his.

And he had no idea what to do with that information, but it was all he could think about.

She looked at him as he pulled onto the road and pointed them toward town.

He dialed his brother.

"Detective Beaumont," Finn said, voice rising from the truck's speakers.

"It's me," Austin said. "You're on speaker, and I'm with Scarlet Wills. She's remembered a few details about her assailant and would like to meet with you if you've got some time."

"Nice," Finn said. "Did she remember what he looks like?"

"Kind of," Scarlet said, answering for herself. "I don't think it'd be worth meeting with a sketch artist, but I might be able to pick him out in a lineup."

"Can y'all meet me at the station in about twenty minutes?" Finn asked. "I'm headed that way now."

"Not a problem," Austin said.

"Good. Once we have some suspects, we'll call you in for that. How do you feel about taking a look in the mug shot database?"

A bright smile split her pretty face. "I can do that."

"Finn," Austin said. "Any news on the phone number used to order those flowers yesterday?"

"Unfortunately," he said, "it was a disposable unit like we suspected. Unregistered. I'm still working to track down the prepaid credit card's origin. So we could still get lucky on that."

Austin doubted it. This criminal was proving to be a real planner.

Chapter Thirteen

Scarlet trembled as she crossed the parking lot to the Marshal's Bluff police station. Her body couldn't seem to understand the reason for her recent jolt of adrenaline, and her fight-or-flight response was going haywire.

She took a calming breath with every step and hoped the rush would soon pass. She wanted to thank the detective on her case for all the effort he was making to protect her, and she hoped the news about her attacker's description would help speed up his capture.

She was also eager to talk to another member of Austin's family. Mostly because she was an only child, and siblings had always interested her. Nothing more.

Austin held the door to the lobby for her to pass, then greeted a uniformed officer behind a sliding glass window by name.

The men exchanged a few words while Scarlet took in her surroundings. The space was pleasant, if she didn't get caught up in the fact that everything heavier than a magazine was bolted to the floor.

A nearby buzz set them in motion once more. Austin steered her through another door, one hand on her back.

They passed several offices in a narrow corridor before a ridiculously attractive man in a gray dress shirt, black slacks and a blue tie leaned into the hall ahead of them.

"Hey." His gaze moved from Austin to Scarlet, and recognition hit. This was Detective Beaumont.

Lydia was right. These men came from an unfair gene pool.

"Hey," Austin echoed. "Finn, you remember Scarlet Wills. Scarlet, you've met my little brother Finn."

Finn offered her his hand and she shook it. "I remember. You're looking well. It's nice to see you under better circumstances."

"Thanks," she said, following him into an office. He'd visited her on the night of her attack, but she'd been too out of sorts to hold much of a conversation.

Austin closed the door behind them then motioned for her to take a seat in one of the two chairs in front of his brother's desk.

Finn returned to the rolling chair on the other side.

She hadn't noticed before, but the resemblance between brothers was profound. Brown hair and eyes. Straight noses and teeth. Broad shoulders and square jaws.

Finn swiveled an open laptop to face her. "This is our mug shot database. It's fairly easy to navigate. You input the things you know here." He pointed to a set of drop-down lists on the left side bar. "Then click search."

Like online shopping, she thought. Except instead of

sorting by price or pattern, she'd set the physical characteristics she wanted to see.

"It helps to sort by known offenses," he said. "Since we don't know if this guy has a criminal record, we'll have to work with what we've got. In the event he's never been arrested, this exercise will be futile, but at least it's somewhere to start."

Scarlet made a few selections and clicked search.

Finn slid a pad of paper and pen across the desk to her. "It might also be helpful to list all the men you see regularly or would recognize if you saw them on the street. Specifically those who live in town or nearby."

She straightened. "Like coworkers and clients? Or the barista at Java Jim's and the clerk at the grocery?"

"All of the above," Finn said. "Dry cleaner, mailman, guys from your gym. Anyone you've interacted with in the time since this began, or just before you started feeling watched. Even a simple exchange, a polite word or smile can be misconstrued as interest to these types of perpetrators."

She pursed her lips, hating that idea. She spoke to dozens of people every day. "Okay."

She switched gears, pulling the paper closer and starting a list while faces appeared in her mind like popcorn. She began with real estate agents and clients, then moved on to groundskeepers, bank representatives and title clerks, the man who cleaned the office, and a handful of workers at businesses she frequented. "You won't tell all these people I named them as potential criminals, will you?"

Finn chuckled. "No. And feel free to flag the ones

you're sure don't fit the physical description. I'll still want to talk to them in case we're looking for some-one peripherally connected."

She wrote until her hand cramped and she'd ex-hausted the list inside her brain. Then she returned the paper to Finn and her attention to the database search results.

"This is good," he said. "Thank you."

"Mom stopped by," Austin said.

Finn snorted a small laugh. "I had no doubt she would."

"She brought food."

"Uh-huh."

The brothers dove headlong into a discussion on their allegedly meddling mother, whom Scarlet thought was lovely. So she quickly tuned them out.

Her attacker's shadowed face, the hoodie and beard played on a loop in her mind. Little flashes. Tiny pieces of a larger picture. And something more. There was something about his mouth. She tried to hold on to the image for inspection. His lips hadn't been snarled or curled in anger as he'd choked her. The ex-pression was flat, resigned. As if his strangling Scar-let was merely necessary. Something he simply had to do so he could go home and get on with his night.

She shivered, wondering what he was doing now. Was he afraid he'd soon be caught? Or did he like the chase? *Maybe*, she thought, *he's eating a hamburger with friends at the sports bar down the street*. Com-pletely unaffected by what he'd done.

She forced her attention back to the screen where

she'd been mindlessly scrolling. How many photos had she missed?

None of the faces before her now seemed right, and the more she scrolled, the more uncertain she became. Maybe she wouldn't recognize him after all.

A ringing phone broke her concentration once more.

The Beaumonts stilled as well, but no one made a move to answer the call.

A long moment seemed to pass before she realized the ringing phone belonged to her.

"Oh!" She pulled the device from her jacket pocket, having completely forgotten she'd tucked it in there when she left Austin's truck.

Her heart sank as she looked to the screen.

"Who is it?" Austin asked, swiveling on his seat with interest.

A reasonable question, considering she'd only had the phone for an hour or so, and she didn't even know its number. She did, however, recognize the digits on-screen.

"It's my mother."

AUSTIN WATCHED AS Scarlet's expression moved from confusion to astonishment, then resignation as she answered the call. She scanned Finn's small office, likely seeking but not finding anyplace for privacy.

Finn raised his brows, noticing Austin's interest. He shrugged.

"Hello, Mom," Scarlet said, turning slightly away. "I'm fine. How did you get this number?" A soft groan left her lips. "Lydia."

Finn knocked gently on the desk, returning Austin's attention to him once more. "Is she close to her mama?"

He nodded. "I think it's the reason she's been putting this off. She called her office earlier. Lydia must've passed the number along."

Finn cringed. "Can you imagine if that was our mama?"

Austin matched his expression. "No."

"I'm serious," Scarlet said. "I'm barely injured. I was only kept for observations. A bump on the head and some bruising." She rubbed a hand over her eyes. "I asked them if they wanted to reschedule, and Lydia's handling the ones who don't."

Austin frowned. Had her mama moved on to shop-talk in the span of a couple sentences?

"Mom," Scarlet said, voice firming on the single syllable. "I'm at the police station right now, and I need to go so I can concentrate. We're trying to identify the man who did this." She glanced at the Beaumonts.

Austin and Finn looked at one another, both caught silent and staring.

"No, I don't need you to come to Marshal's Bluff. I'm staying with a friend for a few days...Because I didn't want to bother you."

Finn tented his brows. "Who's the friend?"

"Me." Austin slid his gaze away. "We might stay at my place until I can get her locks changed."

"We?"

"Yes," Austin said under his breath, returning his attention to his brother. "Obviously."

"When did y'all become a we?" Finn whispered back.

Austin scowled. "What?"

Finn raised his palms and leaned farther in his brother's direction. "You could've said you invited her to your place, or that she agreed to stay with you for now. You didn't have to use the word *we*. But you did."

"That's ridiculous." Austin mouthed the words.

"Sorry," Scarlet said, sliding the phone into her coat pocket. "That was my mom."

Finn dragged his gaze away from Austin and worked up a polite smile. "I hope she wasn't too worried."

"She took it better than expected," Scarlet said. "Of course, I didn't give her a lot of details, and apparently she hasn't looked online. Lydia said the morning paper covered things pretty well."

"It did indeed," Finn said. "Normally I would've played this close to the vest, but in your case I felt it was best to make an offensive move over a defensive one. By announcing this man's out there strangling women, folks will be cautious and vigilant. Hopefully people will be talking about him everywhere he goes and the spotlight will put a dent in his confidence."

She blinked. "You're trying to rattle him?"

"I want to make him think twice before acting out again. I need time to review all the materials related to this case, and considering how involved you are in the community, there are a lot of interviews to conduct." He lifted his notepad and turned it in her direction. "You have interactions with so many people on a regular basis that you broke them into categories. And each of these names is more than a potential suspect, it's a link." He looked at the paper then back to Scarlet. "You order coffee from Dustin a few days a week at Java Jim's, but when I talk to him, I might learn there's a cook in back on the days you normally visit, and a pastry delivery is also made around that time. Then I need to talk to the cook and pastry guy too."

She slumped in her chair. "So my list of fifty names could lead you to speak with a hundred people."

"Yep, and I can't have your attacker lashing out while I'm still doing the preliminary data collection."

"What if he gets a thrill from everyone talking about him?" she asked. "Like those bombers and pyromaniacs who stand around the crime scene, enjoying the trouble they caused."

"Right now, I'm willing to let his ego inflate a little, especially if that means he's not out there looking for you."

Austin rested a palm against the side of her chair, wishing he could squeeze her hand instead. "You okay? We can always come back later if you're getting tired or sore. Finn's got a nice long list of people to talk to now. He can use that to get started."

She looked to the screen then back. "Give me a few more minutes?"

"Sure."

He watched as she pushed herself to refocus. Then he dropped his hands into his lap and faced his brother. "Anything I can do to help you? I'll be at my place for a few days laying low, but I can research."

Finn worked his jaw, eyes seeking and hands clasped on the desk. "I'll let you know. Maybe I'll send you a copy of this list." He tapped the notepad. "Right now, you've got a witness to protect."

"Thank you," Scarlet said, still scrolling through mug shots. "For calling me a witness. Not a victim."

Finn opened his mouth then closed it and grunted.

Austin grinned. Scarlet Wills was a lot of things, but she wasn't a victim.

Eventually, her recent injuries got the best of her and she began to squirm, tipping her head side to side, stretching her neck and kneading her shoulders.

Austin nudged her with an elbow. "Let's go. You've done enough today, and we can always come back."

She sighed and slumped against the chair. "Yeah, okay."

Finn walked them down the hall and bid his farewell, leaving Austin to escort her back to his truck.

"You did a good job today," he said. "Did I tell you?"

She smiled. "I think I might've heard that."

"What do you think about getting that glass of wine and watching the sunset from my deck tonight?"

Her eyes lit. "You have a deck?"

"I do."

"And wine?" she asked.

He beeped his truck doors unlocked. "I've got hard cider. It's fruity, so that's a little like wine. Right?"

"Wine adjacent," she said. "I accept."

"Then let's call it a day. We can spend the rest of the afternoon relaxing in a pair of rockers like retirees."

A sharp whistle turned Austin toward the police department before she could respond.

Finn jogged in their direction as Austin opened the passenger door for Scarlet. "Wait. I just got a call from Dispatch. A fire was reported at 1611 Inlet Way. The fire department is already en route."

Austin's eyes snapped to Scarlet.

She gasped. "That's my place!"

Chapter Fourteen

Scarlet sat numbly in the passenger side of Austin's truck as they raced through town, hot on Finn's tail. The detective's lights and sirens parted traffic for him, and Austin glided his truck through in the wake, like the second line to the world's worst parade.

Austin used voice commands to call Dean and a few others, attempting to get information about how bad the situation was, but everyone was still en route as they were.

Scarlet kneaded her hands, certain some part of her would die if her home was unsalvageable. She'd put her heart and soul into the restoration of the property, not to mention most of her money. Those walls were her safe haven. No amount of insurance money could rebuild it. The structure was historic. And some modern throwback or replica would never be the same.

Worrying about installing the wrong doorknobs seemed incredibly trivial when the place was on fire.

"We're arriving now," an unfamiliar male voice explained through the truck speakers. The sound of waning sirens faded in the background. "No visible flames," he said. "What's your ETA?"

"Three minutes," Austin reported. "See you soon."

The call disconnected, and Scarlet stared at his face. "Who was that?" she asked. "What did he mean? No visible flames. There's no fire?"

"Mark's a volunteer EMT. We'll know what he meant soon."

She swallowed a lump of fear rising in her throat and fixed her gaze outside the windshield.

The fire trucks were first to come into view. One had parked in her driveway. Another along the roadside. A police cruiser and an ambulance were angled into the space between the trucks.

"Someone called 911," Austin said. "I'm guessing it was the same person who set the fire, wanting to make sure you got the call while you were out and had to hurry back and find all this madness."

All Scarlet cared about in the moment was that Austin's friend had been right. There weren't any flames visible from the road. She placed a hand over her heart and sent up prayers of gratitude.

Austin parked behind the first responders. "Let's see what these guys know."

She hopped out and met him at the front bumper then hurried in the direction of her home.

Finn had jammed his vehicle into her driveway behind the first fire truck, two of his wheels on her lawn. He spoke to a passing fireman on his way to meet Austin and Scarlet. "We're going to get an update and report in a minute. Whatever happened in there, it looks like he's escalating again. I'm glad you made plans to stay elsewhere for a while."

Austin curved his fingers around hers, offering a small squeeze. "Do we have any idea how bad it looks inside?"

Scarlet's mind reeled. Fire could've ruined, charred or weakened the internal structure. There could be irrevocable smoke damage. Or chemical and water damage caused by whatever was done to stop the flames and smoke from spreading.

"Escalating," she said, repeating Finn's word. Her voice sounded foreign to her ears.

The word rolled in her mind, circling and itching.

"Yeah," Finn said. "And this is exactly the kind of lashing out I'd hoped to avoid."

Austin tugged her hand gently. "Are you okay? Scarlet?"

The Beaumonts' words sounded as if they were underwater. Flashes of her attacker holding her in place whipped in and out of her mind. *He is escalating.*

"I think he spoke to me," she said.

"Who?" Finn asked.

She shook her head, unwilling to be sidetracked as she clung to the sensation of her attacker's hands on her mouth and middle. "He whispered something into my ear when he pressed his cheek to mine." She closed her eyes, imagining the scratch of his whiskers, and her lids flew open. "He said he wanted us to be together." She looked from Finn to Austin, heart racing and stomach souring. "Something like that. There's more, but I can't—"

The brothers exchanged a look.

Scarlet's fuzzy thoughts suddenly cleared. Wasn't escalation supposed to move more slowly? "When I came to you, I thought I was being followed," she told Austin. "You said it was possible that had been going on for weeks. Then out of nowhere, he attacked me. Now two days later he lit my home on fire. It feels more like he's unraveling."

Austin rubbed his forehead then the back of his neck. "I think he saw you with me and became territorial. The attack might've been the warning you mentioned. Maybe that's why he let you live."

Her mouth twisted in disgust. "Then he tried to apologize by sending flowers."

"But I was there, and I called him."

Finn hooked his hands on his hips. "I'm guessing by all this." He motioned to the abundance of emergency vehicles surrounding her property. "He knows Austin spent the night here last night."

Nausea twisted in Scarlet's core. What if the person who'd set a fire in her home while she was away had acted last night instead? When she was sleeping and Austin was circling her home, trying to watch both doors by himself.

She stepped away from Austin and wrapped one arm around her middle, covering her mouth with the other hand.

A fireman strode in their direction, and Finn stepped forward with an outstretched hand. "How does it look in there?"

Their small circle turned expectantly.

The fireman made eye contact with her, then Austin, nodding to each, before returning his attention to the detective. "Small fire. No damage."

"I don't understand," she said. How could there be a fire without damage?

The fireman glanced over his shoulder at her house. "It appears as if a contained fire was intentionally started in the master bedroom. Nothing else seems amiss. It's safe to go inside and take a look when you're ready."

Finn tipped his head. "After you."

Austin turned to Scarlet, but her feet felt like lead.

He slid his hand in hers once more and gave that familiar, gentle squeeze. "Scarlet." He dipped his head closer. "I've got you."

Then they were in motion.

First responders milled around, chatting and watching as Scarlet and Austin passed. This small, contained fire was sure to be tomorrow's front-page news. It probably wouldn't take long for the dark cloud to settle over her name as a Realtor. The lady with a stalker. A bad luck human to be avoided. Then where would she be?

She'd have to start over. Again.

A million unkind words flooded into her mind. Nasty comments from her mother's many companions, snide words from Scarlet's former boyfriends. Unkind teachers who'd assumed she was the problem when her dyslexia made it harder for her to learn new material, before she'd gotten the help she'd needed.

Anyone and everyone in her past who'd seemed to believe all their problems started and ended with her.

She'd overcome a lot of those burdens with regular trips to the therapist and remediation training for her dyslexia, but she was sixteen and miserable again as she marched into her home. Even with Austin at her side.

"No signs of forced entry," an officer stated to Finn as he reached the porch. The man in uniform nodded to her as she passed.

"He has my keys," Scarlet said, mostly to herself. There wasn't any reason to break in now. And if the criminal lost her keys, he could always use a credit card to gain access.

She followed the parade of men into her bedroom where another person in uniform took photos of the metal bucket, normally used to collect ashes from the living room fireplace. Now seated on her bed. Black soot marks marred the beautiful eyelet cover.

"Books were used to kindle the fire," the fireman said, pointing to the bucket. "A liquid accelerant enhanced the flames. Smoke detectors were going off when we arrived."

Finn made a path from one side of her bed to the other. "Who called this in?"

The fireman shrugged.

Scarlet supposed Finn already knew that answer, and the number was likely tied to another untraceable, disposable phone. "He wanted me to know he was angry," she said, feeling as if she was finally catch-

"One Minute" Survey

You get up to **FOUR** books <u>and</u> a Mystery Gift...

ABSOLUTELY FREE!

YOU pick your books – WE pay for everything!

See inside for details.

YOU pick your books –
WE pay for everything.
You get up to FOUR new books and a Mystery Gift... absolutely FREE!
Total retail value: Over $20!

Dear Reader,

Your opinions are important to us. So if you'll participate in our fast and free "One Minute" Survey, YOU can pick up to four wonderful books that WE pay for when you try the Harlequin Reader Service!

As a leading publisher of women's fiction, we'd love to hear from you. That's why we promise to reward you for completing our survey.

IMPORTANT: Please complete the survey and return it. We'll send your Free Books and a Free Mystery Gift right away. And we pay for shipping and handling too! *We pay for EVERYTHING!*

Try **Harlequin® Romantic Suspense** and get 2 books featuring heart-racing page-turners with unexpected plot twists and irresistible chemistry that will keep you guessing to the very end.

Try **Harlequin Intrigue® Larger-Print** and get 2 books featuring action-packed stories that will keep you on the edge of your seat. Solve the crime and deliver justice at all costs.

Or TRY BOTH!

Thank you again for participating in our "One Minute" Survey. It really takes just a minute (or less) to complete the survey… and your free books and gift will be well worth it!

If you continue with your subscription, you can look forward to curated monthly shipments of brand-new books from your selected series, always at a discount off the cover price! Plus you can cancel any time. So don't miss out, return your One Minute Survey today to get your Free books.

Pam Powers

ing up, but very late to the game. "Another warning. Not a punishment."

The final word stuck in her head and itched in her throat. Another memory hovered just out of reach. Another awful thought pushed the curiosity aside.

The man who'd nearly killed her had been in her home while she was away. He'd been in her bedroom. Invaded her space, used her keys as if he belonged there. And for those reasons, this threat felt inexplicably more personal than the physical attack. If nothing more had gone wrong, she might've been able to convince herself she'd been in the wrong place at the wrong time when she was strangled. But there wasn't any way to deny this threat was intended for one person. This was absolutely about her.

Finn and the firemen left her room.

She turned to watch them go, having missed whatever they'd said.

Austin stepped closer. He released her hand in favor of sliding his palms along her forearms. "How are you doing?"

She exhaled a thin breath. "Not good."

He pulled her against him for a quick hug. "They have one more thing to show us, then you can gather your things and we'll get out of here."

Scarlet straightened and followed him through her open bedroom door.

Finn and the fireman stood before a small built-in desk in her parlor. Floor-to-ceiling bookshelves stood on either side. Several tomes were missing. Likely the ones used to start the fire.

A photo of Scarlet in a long white beaded gown centered her small desk. Her image beamed back at them. The gown had been spectacular, rented from one of those big LA shops and returned when the event had ended. The plunging neckline and slit up one side had made her feel confident and sexy.

The party had been amazing, attended by top real estate agents, bank execs and related industry stars. All to see her and a handful of others receive awards for excellence.

"When was this taken?" Finn asked.

"Last summer," she said, then thought better of it. "Not a few months ago," she clarified. "The year before. Maybe fifteen months back. It was a banquet thrown by Coulter Realty executives."

Finn stretched blue gloves over his hands and lifted the photo. "Fifteen months, huh?"

A slip of paper scooted across the desk in the picture's absence, revealed and set free by Finn's action.

The air thickened, and Scarlet's chest grew tight as she stared at the message and read the tidy script.

You betrayed me.

Chapter Fifteen

Austin spent the next half hour with his fists clenched and jaw set, taking in every comment and detail traded between Finn and the other officials. Hoping to hear some magic words that would give the stalker's identity away.

Scarlet had excused herself to collect her things and probably do some internal screaming.

The simmering rage was real and very thinly veiled, for him at least.

He'd promised to be her eyes and ears, so she wouldn't miss anything while she packed.

Eventually, the fire trucks and ambulance took their leave, carrying the first responders with them. Finn and his team stayed a bit longer, attempting to pull fingerprints from the doorjambs and knobs, as well as the desk, bookshelves and the fireplace bucket.

Austin hoped they'd find something but suspected they wouldn't. Whoever they were dealing with was meticulous. Worse, Scarlet said he'd worn leather gloves to attack her. He'd likely worn them for this as well.

Finn leaned against the archway between Scarlet's

living room and kitchen. "I'm going back to the station," he said. "I need food and a little time to make sense of the information we have. Hopefully I can get it to lead somewhere."

"Good luck," Austin said, meaning it to his core.

"Thanks. I'm just glad he continues to leave clues." Finn sighed and tented his brows. "It's obvious I don't have to say this, but I will anyway."

Austin frowned.

"Keep her close." Finn flicked his gaze over Austin's shoulder, presumably toward the room where Scarlet was packing. "I know you like to get involved and take action. We all do, but this time your energies will be best used to entertain her. Distract her. Keep her away from town."

Finn was right. That didn't need saying.

Austin bit his tongue and nodded.

Finn released a small puff of air and rolled his shoulders. "I know you know what you're doing, but it's also my job to say the words. Speaking as your brother now," he said, voice lowering drastically. "She's hurting, scared and hunted. This situation could become an issue."

Austin crossed his arms and straightened. "You don't think I can protect her?" Was he kidding?

"That's not what I'm concerned about."

Austin narrowed his eyes, and the brothers exchanged a long silent look.

He imagined Finn was attempting to telepathically point out that Scarlet was vulnerable and Austin wasn't the sort to get serious about a woman, yet he'd been seen holding her hand by half the emergency responders in town. And that could be confusing for many people.

Knowing he'd probably think the same things in Finn's shoes, he settled for a curt dip of his chin.

Finn relaxed, glanced around the home then headed for the door. "Call if you need anything."

"Back at you," Austin said, following. "Keep us in the loop if something new comes up. Even a small thing. We want to know."

Finn stopped on the porch to puff out his cheeks. "We." He shook his head then jogged to his truck and climbed inside.

Austin stared after him. He had started thinking of himself and Scarlet as a we. He didn't want to think about why. It wouldn't end well. His relationships never did. Other than his mama, all the women he knew took issue with his job. It kept him out too late, gone too long and unable to discuss what he'd been up to most of the time. Since he couldn't imagine doing anything else for a living, he'd stopped trying to find a significant other.

A small crash in the next room set Austin in motion, heading toward the source of the sound.

Scarlet stood before her dresser, picking up a collection of books she'd apparently dropped while packing.

He crouched to help, but his heart stopped at the sight of her.

Tears tracked over her cheeks. Her eyes were glossy, her face pink.

They stood at the same time, and she wiped her face. "Sorry. I'm a little shaky, and I thought I had them stacked better."

He stepped forward without thinking and pulled her into his arms. A bad habit he couldn't seem to break. "You don't have to apologize. Let me help you."

"No. I've got it." She edged away, face cleared of emotion. "I'm ready." She tucked the books into a bag on her bed then lifted the handle of a large suitcase. "This looks like a lot, but it's not all clothing. I'm bringing some of the smaller things I wouldn't want destroyed in a fire if he comes back."

Austin pressed his lips together, feeling irrationally rejected by the way she'd pulled away. He'd crossed a line by hugging her, and he needed to be more professional. "It's no problem. Bring as much as you want."

He made a mental note to keep a more polite distance moving forward. He wouldn't allow her to be hurt again on his watch. Not by the criminal currently tormenting her. And certainly not by himself.

Scarlet bounced along in Austin's truck, moving away from town and the sea. It was strange to her, not to live near the water. But he'd grown up on a ranch, so maybe it wasn't as important to him as it was to her. Still, she'd be even more of a mess than she was if not for her deck and the inlet views to calm her.

The reaching limbs of ancient trees stretched over them, crowding the sky into little more than a pale blue ribbon above. The narrow gravel road ahead was spattered with autumn leaves in every color and utterly devoid of other vehicles.

He glanced at her as the truck waddled along, more and more slowly as the path they traveled grew infinitely less accommodating of their apparent trespass. "Are you worried yet?"

She dared a look in his direction, then returned her eyes to the road, if that's what she was supposed to call it. "Have I wondered if I accidentally let a serial killer drive me into the mountains to escape a stalker? Nope. That's never crossed my mind."

Austin chuckled, and the road began to smooth. Fresh chunks of gray gravel led to a short, covered bridge, then bent around another corner in the distance. Every board of the bridge appeared new.

"Wow." She leaned forward, admiring the structure. "There aren't many covered bridges left in North Carolina. What on earth is one doing here?"

"My brothers and I put it here," he said. "With a little help from our dad. It took us more than a decade."

She turned to gape at him.

He rolled onto the bridge's center and shifted into park. "Do you want to get out and look?"

"Absolutely." She climbed down and ran her hands over the treated wood, taking in the obvious craftsmanship. "You really built this?"

His smile was proud as he approached. "We started when I was a kid. My grandma owned the land, and she liked covered bridges. She had a lot of memories of the one in the town where she grew up. Grandpa proposed there. So, when she was getting older, Dad made her foreman on this project, and he enlisted my brothers and I for free labor. We took turns leaving for the military and college, but eventually we got the job done."

"And your grandma?"

He shook his head. "She was around for most of it, but she was too ill to see it finished. We promised to bring her here on the next nice day, but she passed during the winter. I guess it wasn't meant to be."

Scarlet moved to his side and folded her hands in front of her, determined not to touch him like she wanted. All the touching only made things more confusing. "I'm sorry you lost your grandma. She must've felt so loved, seeing you do this for her." Scarlet couldn't imagine. The possibility love like that existed, even between a grandparent and their grandchildren, tightened her lungs and filled her heart with hope.

"I like to think so," he said. "She was very special to us all."

Scarlet moved to the bridge's edge, drawn by the sounds of running water. "I can't believe your dad knew how to do this. And that he was able to teach children."

"Grandpa was a carpenter. Dad learned a lot growing up with him, and we learned a lot working with Dad. Our family didn't always have tangibles to pass down, like family jewels or antique whatnots. But our parents and grandparents did what they could to give us their morals, values and skills."

She rested her hands on the wide railing and peered

through a cutout in the bridge's side. Initials had been carved into the wood. D.B., F.B., A.B., L.B., J.B. She traced the set in the center. "Is J.B. your dad?"

"My oldest brother, Jake."

She wondered which face was Jake's in the family photo at Austin's office, but the image had already faded in her mind.

Below them, water burbled over rocks and around fallen trees, cutting an arched path through the hillsides. A hundred yards ahead, on the freshly graveled road, stood an old mill, its waterwheel motionless in the creek.

Austin leaned a hip against the railing. "These aren't quite inlet views, but they make me happy when I've had a tough day."

She turned to squint at him. "You live nearby?"

He hitched his chin toward the mill. "Grandma left the property to me. My brothers got other things. They wouldn't have wanted this, and I wouldn't have wanted anything else."

"And you live here now?" she asked, attempting to make sense of it.

He nodded. "I'm restoring the place a little at a time. I'll have the rest of the road repaired and covered with gravel in the spring. Living back here is the main reason I keep my old truck. I've never gone anywhere it couldn't take me."

Scarlet smiled, fitting another piece of the Austin Beaumont puzzle into place. She already knew he loved his family, history and the outdoors. Now she knew he was good with his hands.

He smiled, and her face heated. "Are you cold?" he asked, likely mistaking the color in her cheeks.

She shrugged, unwilling to lie and not trusting her mouth while her brain felt a little on the fritz.

"Let's go inside." He opened her door and waited while she climbed in. Then he drove the rest of the way to his home.

The former mill was a two-story rectangle with a triangular roof, like the ones children draw on paper. Weathered old boards ran lengthwise like a log cabin, making up the body of the structure. Red metal panels replaced the original roof. Thick beds of black mulch and a row of brightly colored mums lined the brick walkway. A grapevine wreath with a burlap bow hung on the painted black door.

"Pretty," she said, climbing steps cut from stone as old as time.

"Mama decorates everything," he said, unlocking and opening the door. "She says pretty things put folks at ease."

"She's not wrong," Scarlet said, following him inside.

Battered hardwood floors spread out before them to an exposed brick wall. A small table sat against the stone with a framed sketch of the mill hanging above and an empty vase. A set of steps anchored the wall to her left. A pass-through arch in the bricks drew her forward.

The space beyond was wholly unfinished, covered in dust and fallen plaster from a crumbling ceiling.

A row of tall, skinny windows lined the far wall and overlooked the waterwheel.

"This will eventually be my office," Austin said, motioning to a set of sawhorses topped with a sheet of wood and a stack of files. A ladder-back chair stood behind it. "Come on. Let's get you settled upstairs."

He led her up the sturdy, visibly reinforced staircase, past strips of insulation rolled between two-by-fours. Clearly a work in progress with much more to be done.

She began to worry about what she'd find on the second floor.

Those fears subsided as she rounded the bend in the stairs.

A spacious, open floor plan rolled out before her. On this level, the exposed bricks from below became a fireplace dividing the studio. A small island stood before multiple sets of French doors overlooking a rear deck. Stainless steel appliances and painted cabinets hugged the corner, careful not to interrupt the view. Living room furniture had been arranged on an earthen-colored rug before the fireplace, and a large bed with scrolled iron head and footboards anchored the wall opposite the creek views.

"There's only one bedroom and bathroom," he said. "I can set up a cot in my office or sleep on the couch if you're okay with me being up here. You're welcome to the bed, and the bath is around the corner there." He pointed.

She stared, trying to reconcile what lay before her with the exterior views and the barely passable road.

He frowned. "You don't like it."

"No. I love it. It's like living in a tree house." A really modern, very cool tree house.. She moved to the bank of glass doors, mouth hanging unashamedly agape. "How do you ever make yourself leave?"

"I'm money motivated. I like to eat and keep the lights on. Plus, there's a lot still to be done here, and that all takes cash."

"Have you applied for historical property grants?"

He smiled. "I have. I might be able to get some help with restoration of the wheel and road, but not the mill. I've altered too many things, and the updates have negated eligibility."

She gazed at the granite countertop and Edison lights over the island. She supposed he had changed a lot, but the structure was still original. Wasn't it? Not the roof. Her mind whirled with new purpose. Maybe when her stalker was jailed, she could help Austin look for available funds.

Assuming he wanted to remain friends.

Austin's stomach growled, and she grinned.

"I don't suppose you get pizza delivery here?"

"No." He moved toward the fridge and opened the doors. "But I've got a grill and some free time. How do you feel about burgers?"

"I feel very good about burgers," she assured him.

And Austin went to work.

Chapter Sixteen

They sat on Austin's deck long after the meal was finished and the sun dipped low in the sky. Scarlet actively reminded herself that the last few days, and the current moment, were real. She wasn't dreaming and wouldn't wake up to her formerly predictable and satisfying life. That era was over. It wasn't safe to go home.

Austin excused himself and returned with two brown bottles. "As promised, my special wine."

She smiled as he approached with the hard cider. "Those look perfect for fall."

He twisted the cap from one bottle and passed it her way. "What?"

"What?" she repeated, accepting the offer.

"You made a face when I took off the cap. I'm sure you could've done it yourself. I was just being—"

"Kind," she said. "I know. I'm starting to pick up on the pattern."

He returned to the rocking chair at her side. "I've noticed some of your routines too."

"Like?"

"You frown a lot when anyone does anything for

you. The simplest things. Like when Finn held the door. Or Mama brought breakfast. When I breathe."

She smiled and took a sip of her cider. "Habit. I'm not used to the help, I guess. I've been on my own a long time, and I don't have siblings or close friends. So I just do everything myself."

He looked offended.

She bristled. "There's nothing wrong with being self-sufficient. Don't look like I just told you I hate your truck."

He kicked back in the chair, swigging from his bottle before speaking. "What about your mama? You must've been her top priority, since it was just the two of you."

Scarlet debated her response. She hated talking about herself, and especially about her life before moving to Marshal's Bluff. But she also longed for someone in her life she could be real with. *And if Austin has a problem with my truth, he doesn't have to stick around when this is over*, she reasoned.

She watched the water flowing through the creek below, letting it soothe her nerves and urge her on. Maybe it was time to be transparent for a change. Time to stop putting on a show. Everything else was changing. Why not this too? Besides, she was almost certain Austin wouldn't hold her past or secrets against her. If not because he was genuinely honorable, then because she'd soon be out of his life if that was what he wanted.

He waited patiently while she chose her words.

"My mom started selling homes when I was in elementary school. I don't remember much about my dad, but after he moved out, she told me he only came back to ask her for money, and we didn't have any. He'd threaten to take me with him sometimes, and Mom would empty her tiny bank account for him. She said whatever amount she had was always enough to make him go away, but never enough for a lawyer."

Austin's jaw flexed. Unhappy or uncomfortable. She couldn't be sure which, but he'd asked, so she was answering.

"When Mom heard how much money she could earn selling houses, she made it her mission to be the very best agent she could. We drove all day once, visiting every thrift store in three counties looking for suits and costume jewelry on the cheap. Then she studied every night after her shifts at the diner and got her real estate license. She was my age then, beautiful, witty, motivated. She did well and made a shrewd businesswoman. I never doubted I'd follow in her footsteps."

"Why do I sense a but?" he asked. "I know you sell real estate."

Scarlet inhaled deeply and released it slowly. "She was busy making a living and thriving on the attention that comes with mastering something, and I was home alone more often than not. I was rarely her priority, but I couldn't complain without feeling guilty because I knew I was the reason she worked so much. She was making ends meet for me. But she was never very…maternal. She did the best she could, and I doubt she has any idea she could've done better."

"You raised yourself and ended up caring for her too," he guessed.

"I did what I could, which wasn't much while I was small, but I got older and I learned. She hired a lawyer to protect me from my dad in the times he was out of jail and on the take." Scarlet forced herself to meet Austin's eyes, waiting for the judgment that came when anyone found out one of her parents had been in jail.

He nodded in understanding, processing without judgment. So, she carried on.

"I was in high school when I discovered I had dyslexia. Until a kind and attentive young teacher caught it, everyone else just thought I wasn't very smart, or that the girl with the uninvolved mom didn't try. By that time, I'd already decided who I was, and I wasn't proud of her. And Mom's continued absence seemed to say I wasn't worth the time. Having dyslexia made it all worse, because once I'd been diagnosed, I couldn't just pretend my grades were low because I was too cool to care. Everyone knew my grades were low because something was wrong with me. I didn't want a label, and I hated being pulled out of class for extra help. I tried to quit school my junior year. Mom wasn't having that, so I rebelled however I could and our relationship suffered for a while."

"Rebelled?" he asked.

"Endlessly." She smiled a little at the lengths she'd gone to push back at a life she thought had pushed her too far. "I got a fake ID, then a tattoo and piercings. I dyed my hair jet-black then cut it off. I skipped classes, and some nights I didn't come home. And I always dated the wrong kinds of men."

Austin rocked in his chair, head turned to face her, the picture of ease. "I'm not going to pretend to know what it's like to be you, then or now. But I will say I grew up on a ranch for troubled youths, and what you've described is practically troubled teen 101. Kids try to regain control however they can. My brothers and I all did similar things too."

She frowned. "Sure."

"We did," he assured her. "We didn't even have it rough in life. We just hated rules and authority. And living on a ranch for struggling kids put a spotlight on us. There was pressure to be some kind of models for appropriate teen behavior. None of us were good with spotlights."

She tried to imagine the pressure he described and wondered if it wasn't easier for her in the house alone. No one caring if she slipped up. She probably would've failed her teen years either way. "I think I dated bad boys to goad my mom. It never worked, and I wound up wanting them to care about me, but they didn't."

"You were young, angry and trusted the wrong people," he said. "Then those people perpetuated your low self-image."

She looked away, hating the truth. "I created my own misery."

"You were a kid, and you were hurting," he corrected. "You turned out pretty great, so it might be worth forgiving yourself."

She opened her mouth to say she already had.

Of course she had. She was twenty-seven years old.
But she couldn't say the words. Because maybe they
weren't true.

"Is it why you listen to so many audiobooks?" he
asked. "Because of the dyslexia?"

"I can read as well as anyone now," she said. "I
like audiobooks because I spend a lot of time in my
car, driving from showing to showing. The books
help pass my time. And I listen at an advanced speed,
which means I read more books a year than I could
otherwise."

Austin took a deep pull from his cider, tipping his
head back as he drank.

Her eyes dropped to the long, tan column of his
throat. Then, a little lower, to the bit of exposed col-
larbone, where his shirt was tugged down at the side.
"I started over when I moved here," she said. "I put
the past behind me, and I began a new story."

"I get that," he said, setting the bottle aside. "You
faced some demons in your teen years and you con-
quered them in your twenties. Sounds like victory
to me."

"I have a tattoo of a broken heart on my hip." She
bit her lip hard, unsure why she'd told him, but need-
ing him to understand her past wasn't behind her—
it was etched into her heart and inked on her skin.

"As far as any men who broke your heart," he said,
shifting forward on his seat and glaring at her. "They
didn't deserve you and probably didn't deserve the
company or attention of anyone, especially a woman.
They probably also had their own emotional issues

and mistreating you made them feel a little bigger. Either way, you weren't the cause of their behavior. That was all on them."

Her eyes stung, and she blinked back the tears. "It's very nice of you to say." No one else ever had.

"It's very true of me to say."

"Why aren't you dating anyone?" she asked, unable to quench her curiosity, and hoping he'd be as candid with her as she had been with him.

Maybe he'd say he hated marriage, believed in open relationships or didn't want kids. Maybe then she could get her head on straight where he was concerned.

He rolled his eyes, looking unprecedentedly self-deprecating. "I live in a small town with three eligible brothers relatively my age. The dating pool got incredibly small, really fast. Aside from that, women don't seem interested in a partner who works long hours, stays out late, often overnight, and can't talk about who he's with or what he's doing."

"So you aren't opposed to dating?"

"No." A small smile played on his lips. "Why? Are you asking?"

She laughed. "It's just good to know there's at least one nice guy out there, willing to treat a partner right."

Austin made a disgruntled sound. "There are lots and lots of men like that. You found the bad ones because you were in a bad place. Those guys were the exceptions, not the rule. I promise you. Now you've got me rethinking my life's mission."

She gave a startled laugh. "You have a life's mission?"

"Don't you?"

She rocked and smiled. "I guess I try to do the best job I can every day at whatever comes my way."

"See?" he said. "And I help and protect anyone I can, however I can. I'm adding you to this list. I will convince you good men exist and there's one out there for you, if you want him."

She wet her lips, hoping that man was him, and not caring that it was silly to want him. Even if they were from two very different upbringings. "You've got lofty goals, Beaumont."

His lips twitched. "More than you know."

Chapter Seventeen

Austin woke groggy and restless the next morning. He hadn't slept well following a long night of research on the potential stalkers in Scarlet's life. And countless replays of his conversation with her before she'd gone to bed.

They'd talked about deep and real things on his deck, things he didn't generally discuss. Not with his friends. Not with his brothers. Absolutely not with someone he'd only known for a few days. Yet, there he was. Scarlet made it so easy to open up, and he could see some of her shared stories had cost her as well. The worst things she'd confided were about her father and the boyfriends of her youth. Too many men had treated her poorly, and those experiences had evidently chipped away at her self-worth. Though no one would know it by talking to her more casually. She hid the dark and bruised parts well. And he wanted more than anything to spend as long as it took to help her heal every past scratch and scrape, because those injuries had nothing to do with her and everything to do with unworthy men.

She'd been especially understanding when he'd shared his reluctance to settle down over the years. He'd been in love once, but she'd had no patience for his work and no trust when he was away. The relationship had gone from the best days of his life to the worst in less than a year. And evoking the fool-me-once motto, he hadn't planned to waste his time, or offer his heart for another punching, ever again.

Scarlet had just nodded and said the whole experience must've been hard.

He'd spent a long while wondering if he was an unintentional hypocrite. He'd insisted Scarlet be open to the possibilities that her bad experiences were exceptions to the rule. Yet he hadn't been willing to take the same chance himself. At least, not before meeting her.

Worse, what if she held him to his challenge? Was he actually supposed to introduce her to someone else so they could fall in love?

His fingers flexed and curled, tempted to knock the hypothetical other guy's lights out.

Living with Scarlet Wills was going to be the death of him.

He sighed in relief when the shower in the next room finally silenced. Knowing she'd been naked and wet on the other side of the wall had conjured a thousand unbidden ideas. The concentration it'd taken to push the thoughts from his mind was exhausting, and he blamed his lack of sleep.

He poured a glass of iced water from his pitcher in the refrigerator and started a fresh pot of coffee. Finn and Dean were on their way over, and they'd likely be exhausted. They too had been working on Scarlet's case long into the night. In fact, everyone he knew with the ability to look for this criminal was on the job and taking it seriously. Austin had never been so thankful for his network of lawmen and related professionals.

The coffee finished brewing several minutes later, and Scarlet still hadn't made an appearance. Something about her prolonged absence struck him as odd.

Maybe he was just looking for a reason to see her sooner, but he went to check on her anyway.

He crossed the floor to his bedroom then rounded the corner to a closed bathroom door.

A low curse and sharp yip sounded inside.

Austin's heart thundered, but he knocked casually. "Everything okay?"

"No!" Scarlet snapped. "It's this ridiculous cut on my shoulder. Of all my injuries, this is the one I hate most."

His muscles tensed. He hated every bump and bruise on her body, but he'd admittedly forgotten about that one. "Are you in pain?" he asked. "Is it bleeding? Should I call your doctor?"

The lock clicked, and the bathroom door crept open. "No. It's healing fine, I think. I just can't reach it to use the cream," she said, shame thick in her voice. "I've only been replacing the bandage for the last couple of days, but it's itchy now, and I have to deal with it. Except I can't."

He looked at the door, now cracked open by an inch, and he imagined her bare shoulder. The long line of her neck, the gentle sway of her hips. The supple fullness of her breasts. He swallowed a groan. The universe was testing him. "Can I help?"

"I feel like a completely helpless human, which I hate," she said. "But yes. Will you please?"

His hand was already on the knob. "Of course."

Scarlet stood inside, looking sheepish and frustrated in a pair of navy blue leggings and a plaid flannel shirt. The buttons at the top were unfastened. She gripped the material at her breastbone, allowing the shirt to drape loosely over her shoulder and down her back. "I can get the bandage on if I prepare it first, then kind of slap it in the right direction, but I can't see what I'm doing to get the cream on. I don't think I could reach it properly, even if I could see."

He stepped inside and closed the door, hoping that would make her feel less exposed. "Just tell me what to do."

She turned her back to him, loosening her grip on the shirt. Their gazes met in the reflection of his bathroom mirror.

An inch or two of slightly puckered skin was visible on one shoulder blade, striped with three small stitches. "It's healing," he said. "That's why it's beginning to itch."

"That's good news, I guess." She sighed, apparently still coming down from her frustration. "I'm supposed to put this cream on the stitches then replace the bandage." She slid a tube of prescription medicine around her middle to him. "The new bandage is set up on the counter, but I can't get this part accomplished."

Austin checked the cluster of materials near his sink. As promised, one square gauze pad was outlined with medical tape and waiting, sticky side up, on the counter. Her shoulder was smeared with the cream nowhere near the wound. "I've got this," he said, smiling at her reflection. "Someone's always injured on the ranch. I've had my fair share of first-aid experience."

"I haven't," she said. "I've never broken a bone, needed my tonsils out or been admitted to a hospital before the other night. I never even needed braces."

He guffawed at her reflection. "Brag a little, why don't you?"

She laughed.

"Hold still." He lifted the tube and squeezed a dollop of cream onto her little wound, thankful the injury wasn't any worse and that the doctor had chosen stitches. Austin had suffered much worse without stitches, but those wounds had left scars. He hated the thought of her being scarred for life by this creep. The emotional and mental aftermath alone would be bad enough. Scarlet didn't need physical reminders too.

Her body swayed closer, leaning back as he gently dabbed at her shoulder, then smoothed the bandage on. He took his time wiping the extra, accidental spots of cream she'd applied before he came to help, and shamelessly savored the feel of her soft, supple skin.

"I'm happy to make this my daily job, if it reduces your stress," he suggested, lingering where he shouldn't.

"I accept," she whispered, relaxing fully against his chest, eviscerating the space between them from hips to shoulders. Her head lolled to one side, and their gazes met in his mirror once more.

Tension ratcheted in him as he watched for signs of uncertainty in her eyes. When he found only curiosity and interest, he stroked his fingers over the curve of her shoulder, tracing her honey-scented skin to the crook of her neck. "Is this okay?"

"Yes." She sighed softly, and his body stiffened.

Austin's heart rate doubled as he thought of a dozen other ways he wanted to touch her and elicit those little sounds. But he was supposed to be her protector. She was hurt, scared and vulnerable. The things he wanted weren't right. At least not right now.

She turned to face him, and his hands fell to his sides. Her chin lifted, and she fixed him with those beautiful moss green eyes. The longing and trust he saw there twisted and tightened his core.

His hands rose again, cupping her hips. He warned himself not to cross a line.

Not to take her mouth with his. Not to toss her unbuttoned shirt and everything else she wore onto the floor so he could worship her. He definitely shouldn't lift her onto the countertop and lose himself inside her.

Scarlet's hands glided over his chest and shoulders, fingertips tangling in his unshorn hair. Her pink lips parted and she rose onto her toes. The slide of her body and warm press of her breasts against him tightened his grip on her hips.

The heat in her gaze set a fire in him, and he felt a fissure form in his already too thin resolve.

"Austin," she whispered, her breath dancing on his lips, inviting them closer.

The sound of his doorbell pushed a curse through his gritted teeth. He forced his hands away from her with the final frayed tether of his self-control. "My brothers are here," he said, voice too deep and gravelly. "Excuse me."

He turned on his toes and headed for the door, forcing his mind and body back into submission with each measured step. And knowing his brothers would still see right through him.

SCARLET STUMBLED BACK, gripping the countertop and wondering what had happened. She'd imagined Austin's mouth on her a thousand times, and she'd practically thrown herself at him in the hopes of experiencing the real thing. But he'd walked away.

Hot, delicious tension seemed to coil around them anytime they were near, and she'd been sure he'd felt it too. She'd spent a long, restless night wondering if the mutual attraction had been only in her mind, but his assistance this morning had been electrified. He'd touched and held her as if he wanted her too.

Hadn't he?

He'd practically run away when the doorbell rang. Actually, he'd cussed first, then run. Had he been upset about the interruption or about what they'd almost done?

The latter seemed silly since he'd offered to find a

good man for her, so she'd see they still existed. When he'd said it, she'd hoped he meant himself. Maybe she'd misread everything. Maybe her confused, over-wrought emotions had made her brain unreliable.

She shook the circling thought away and buttoned her shirt. She left the bathroom with her shoulders square and expression flat.

Male voices rose up the staircase as she moved through the bedroom. "What do you look so guilty about?" someone asked.

She thought the voice might belong to Dean, but she hadn't spoken to him since their initial meeting and phone call.

"I don't know what you're talking about," Austin said.

Was Dean right? Did Austin feeling guilty? Why?

Maybe she'd completely misread it all.

"I've been waiting for you guys," Austin said. "I'm just impatient."

"That doesn't explain the look on your face," Dean pressed. "What happened?"

"What happened to you?" Austin asked. "I don't live that far out of town."

"No, but it's not as if it's easy to get here," Finn answered as a herd of footfalls arrived on the second floor. "Where's Scarlet?"

She waved. "Here."

The brothers stopped in a cluster at the top of the stairs. And they all looked a little guilty in her opinion.

Chapter Eighteen

Dean was first to speak, seeming to break the spell around them. "Hello." He stepped toward her, hand outstretched. "We met at the office. Dean Beaumont."

"I remember," she said, accepting the shake and fighting the urge to more fully cover herself despite the yoga pants and long-sleeved top. She felt exposed, as if all three brothers could see far more than she wanted them to see.

Finn simply raised a hand then slid his eyes at Austin before heading into the kitchen and helping himself to a mug of coffee. Dean followed.

Austin seemed frozen for a long beat.

Scarlet's heart squeezed when their eyes met. Humiliation and confusion heated her cheeks. She'd come on to Austin, and he'd made a polite, but speedy, escape.

Would he ask her to leave now? Maybe send her to his family's farm?

Did his brothers know?

"Looks like you're healing up nicely," Dean said, kindly breaking the silence once more. "How do you feel?"

Scarlet jerked her attention away from Austin and forced a polite smile for the slightly taller, older Beaumont brother. "Thank you." She hadn't noticed how bright his blue eyes were before. After looking into Austin's deep brown gaze for so long, the contrast was slightly jarring. "I'm feeling better. It's been good to get out of town, I think."

Finn unpacked a bag she hadn't noticed him carrying and set up a laptop on the table. "I thought you might want to give the mug shot database another try while I'm here."

She moved in his direction, eager to be useful and glad to have a purpose. The strange energy moving between brothers put her a little on edge. "Sure," she said. "I'd love to."

Finn ran his fingers over the keyboard briefly, then looked at her once more. "All set." He pulled out a chair at the table and motioned for her to sit. "Can I get you some coffee?"

"That sounds nice. Thank you."

The oven dinged, and Dean grabbed potholders from a drawer. "Tell me this is Mama's ham and cheese quiche."

"It is," Austin said, striding stoically into the kitchen to help.

A few minutes later, the four-seat table was covered in plates, mugs and food. And three-quarters of it was surrounded by Beaumonts.

The conversation flowed between small talk and shoptalk seamlessly, each brother easily keeping up as the direction ebbed and flowed, moving in a half dozen directions.

She tried to concentrate on the mug shot database and her coffee. She'd made short work of her breakfast, including two servings of chopped fruit from a bowl.

"I'm hung up on the photo of you in white," Dean said, catching her eye over the laptop's screen. "You looked like a bride."

"Afraid not," she said, glancing up at him. "It was a company event."

Finn shifted. "I've contacted Coulter Realty's home office and asked for a guest list from that night. Can you identify everyone visible in the photo with you? Including folks in the background? It might help us focus our search."

Her knee began to bob beneath the table, unsettled by the implication. "You think it could be someone from my company?"

"Or someone peripherally related, yes."

She wasn't sure why that information made her situation feel worse, but it did.

"Do you commonly use the same service people when you're preparing homes for sale?" Finn asked.

"Frequently." Scarlet took a big drink from her coffee. "We have preferred companies for lawn maintenance, home inspections, stagers, bankers and title companies to name a few. Representatives from all of those companies were at the party, plus Realtors and their guests, event staff and valets."

Dean wiped his mouth with a napkin. "Sounds like a lot of interviews to arrange."

"Will you discount the people from my daily life now?" she asked. "From the list I gave you before the fire?"

"Not completely," Finn said. "I'm just shifting my focus a bit. That photo is significant to your attacker. I want to know why and how he came to have a copy."

"Have you checked online?" she asked. "The company website sometimes uses shots from special events to build the Coulter Realty brand."

"I have, and I didn't see it. I'd like to start contacting the people you remember seeing at the party."

Scarlet nodded, hating that everyone she knew professionally would receive a call from a detective regarding her attack. She returned her focus to the database and soon refilled her coffee.

Dean was the first to leave after breakfast. He offered fist bumps and warm smiles when he headed out. The love and respect between brothers were something she admired. If she'd had siblings, she would've wanted to be their friend too.

Even if her interest in Austin was one-sided, she'd always remember that he showed her what a family could be. And that families like those she read about in books really existed. Because if this existed for the Beaumonts, it could exist for her too one day. That kind of hope was priceless.

Scarlet rubbed her eyes a long while later, tired and stinging from screen fatigue. The mug shots were endless, but she'd begun to wonder if her attacker had ever been arrested. Maybe he was too young. Or too careful. Maybe his stalking tendencies were new, or maybe he'd been content to just watch until now. There were too many unknowns. Too little she could control and too few assurances.

Austin's phone buzzed on the table and Finn's phone rang.

Austin frowned. "Well, that's not good."

"Dean?" Finn asked, phone already at his ear.

Scarlet tensed, hoping nothing bad had happened to their kind, congenial, blue-eyed brother.

Austin stared at his phone then at Finn.

Finn tapped the phone's screen and lowered the device onto the table, speaker function engaged. "Say that again."

"Y'all better come down to our office," Dean said. "I just got here, and there's been trouble."

AUSTIN WAS GETTING tired of following Finn through town from crime scene to crime scene. He hated that all these awful events led back to Scarlet's attacker, and that his office was now involved in something sure to make the paper. Whatever they were driving into this time was a double whammy. Scarlet would be unfairly rattled. And his business would receive bad press.

No one wanted to hire a private investigator everyone was talking about. The most important thing a PI could do was be discreet. But that was out the window now.

He parked his truck along the curb near his office, behind a police cruiser and Dean's truck. A small crowd lined the sidewalk. Several onlookers snapped pictures.

"Take a look at the people," he told Scarlet. She'd barely said ten words to him since asking for help with her bandage this morning, and he needed to apologize, but now wasn't the time. "Let me know if you recognize anyone in the crowd."

"Okay."

"We might want to adjust our plan moving forward," he said, drawing her eyes to his.

"What do you mean?"

"We think this guy was following you for weeks, but he attacked after you met with me. I think he saw us together, either at my office or outside it. Then, he apologized by sending flowers to the hospital, but I called him back and he lost it. I stayed at your house overnight and he lashed out again the next day when we left. He said you betrayed him. There's a pattern forming, and it's not a good one. I think he imagines himself in love with you and doesn't like you spending so much time with me."

"Are you sending me to the farm?" she asked. The words came quick and flat, as if she'd been expecting the possibility to arise.

"No." He frowned. "I won't suggest that again. You want to stay with me, and I want you with me. Now we're making the detail decisions together."

She unbuckled her seat belt and turned on the seat to face him. "Okay. So, what are you suggesting?"

"Maybe we should go out in public as a united front. It might be a good idea to make it clear that I'm not going away soon."

Scarlet chewed her bottom lip. "How?"

"I'd like to stay a little closer to you, if you'd be comfortable with that. Hold your hand, keep you near. Disrupt the misconstrued fantasy that you're his somehow. Make it clear he cannot lay claim to you."

She blinked and scowled. "Like when I tell a guy I'm not interested, but they won't leave me alone until I lie and say I have a boyfriend? Because they have more respect for a fictional boyfriend they've never met than me, the woman they're trying to hit on?"

Austin rubbed a hand against his cheek. "Seriously. We've got to introduce you to nicer people."

The anger bled from her face, replaced by something that looked a lot like hope. "Like you and your brothers?"

"Not my brothers."

Her lips quirked, and the teasing little motion was nearly enough to make him lean in and kiss her.

"About earlier," he said instead. "I'm sorry. I shouldn't have run away."

"I wish you wouldn't have," she whispered.

The urge to kiss her hit again.

Someone rapped on his window, and he turned slowly to see who'd ruined his very pleasant moment.

Dean grinned and waved through the glass. "Are y'all getting out, or did you just come to be near the action?"

Beside him, Scarlet's door opened. She cast a knowing look in his direction as she rounded the hood toward him and his brother.

Austin climbed out as well.

"Ready," she said upon arrival. Then she offered Austin her hand.

He folded his fingers with hers and drew her closer.

"Mama's going to hear about that," Dean muttered, leading the way through the crowd. "Half the people out here know her in one way or another. And everyone knows how she is."

Scarlet stopped short a few paces later, and he did as well.

Big red letters had been spray-painted across the office windows, spelling three familiar words.

SHE IS MINE

Dean stuffed his hands into his pockets. "Our security camera was down, so we don't have any footage of who did this."

Austin struggled to maintain his calm. "What do you mean our cameras were down? That's a top-notch system." He'd made sure of it, chosen every component with exacting care.

"I don't know." Dean frowned, eyes trailing over the red-lettered threat. "It doesn't make any sense. Everything was working fine, then it just…wasn't. At least the glass wasn't broken. The office wasn't breached."

He didn't care about the windows. Those could be replaced. But he loathed the fact that some unhinged, dangerous individual was out there, watching and believing that Scarlet was his. That he had some twisted claim to her. As if she was property instead of a person. And that she was his.

Finn cut through the crowd in their direction,

scratching his head. "One of the officers on my team found a few neighbors near Scarlet's place and the Perez home who are willing to share video footage from their doorbell cameras around the times of those crimes. We'll talk to business owners on this block too. If we're lucky, we might catch the same vehicle near more than one crime scene at the times of the crimes."

Scarlet stared at the big red letters. "This feels less significant than his earlier attacks. Doesn't it? Spray paint instead of fire or destruction."

"Only at first glance," Finn said. "Yes, the person who vandalized the windows could've easily chosen to destroy the office or smash the windows instead, but that destruction would've been open to interpretation. He wanted to leave an exacting message. And it's for Austin this time, not you."

Austin clenched and flexed his jaw. "This is what he said when I called him from the hospital gift shop."

Scarlet squeezed his hand, a small, silent, secret gesture.

And he felt a bit of the tension ease.

"If he's moved on from heartbreak over his imagined loss to rage at Austin for his interference, this could get much worse before it gets any better," Finn said.

Dean snorted a small laugh as his keen gaze drifted over the onlookers. "Keep coming at us, guy. You're only creating more chances to be found."

Austin nodded. He didn't like the idea of a criminal's rage pointed anywhere near Scarlet, but it would certainly help Finn and his team if the stalker continued to lash out. Everything this guy did provided another clue. Another sliver of his identity. And soon the pieces would come together enough to see the big picture.

"Finn?" Scarlet asked.

All eyes in their little circle turned to her. "I thought I was followed away from a home showing the night before I decided to meet with a private investigator. I don't know if it was or wasn't the stalker, but it was a car, not a truck or SUV. I don't know if that will help your team as you review the video footage, but I wanted to say it."

Finn's gaze slid from Scarlet's face to their joined hands. "I'll let the team know." He raised his eyes to Austin and shook his head. "And I can almost guarantee you about five people on this sidewalk have already let Mama know about that."

Dean covered his mouth, failing to hide a wide, toothy smile.

"I've been warned," Austin said.

Scarlet wiggled her fingers, but Austin cupped his free hand over their joined ones and leveled her with a no-nonsense grin. "I'm not worried about Mama, and you don't need to be either."

His brothers broke into laughter and walked away.

Chapter Nineteen

Scarlet rolled her tender shoulders and rubbed the bunching muscles along the back of her neck. Sitting inside the Beaumonts' PI office had red flags of panic flying high in her head, and tension building steadily in her muscles. The last time she'd been here, sitting at this desk, a brutal attack followed, and the trauma from that night sizzled inside her. She might've been followed long before meeting Austin, but it felt as if this was where her nightmare had begun.

Austin placed a bottle of water on the desk before her. "Did you bring your pain pills?"

"Yes." She dug into the small purse she'd brought from home, large enough to carry everything she needed, which was only a phone and pills these days. "Thanks. I almost forgot they existed."

He took a seat on the edge of his desk and watched as she took the medication. "Are you hurting? We can take off anytime if you want to get out of here and lay down. You're supposed to be resting, but I feel as if we're constantly on the move. That must be taking a toll."

"No. I'm okay," she said. "I'd rather be here than somewhere else waiting to know what happened. I can work with facts. The waiting and wondering are worse."

Dean clicked the mouse at his desk, reviewing the feed from their security camera before it went offline. Finn hovered at his side.

Scarlet's phone rang as she tucked the pill bottle back into her purse, and she glanced at the screen. "It's my mom."

Austin nodded and moved to join his brother, giving her space to talk.

"Hey," she answered, forcing enthusiasm she didn't feel into her voice. "How's it going?"

"That's what I called to ask you," her mom said. "I've been thinking of you, and I wondered if you want to come and visit. I can't get out of town because I have a showing first thing tomorrow, but I'm home for the rest of the day, and you said you were taking a little time off, so why don't we meet somewhere for dinner?"

"I'm not sure that's a great idea," she said, gaze flickering to the window washers attempting to scrub the most recent threat off the glass. "The police haven't been able to identify the man who attacked me, and he's making it clear he'll try again."

Her mom was silent.

Finn looked her way, an expression of apology on his handsome face.

She made a mental note to remember she had an audience.

Austin returned to her and waited for acknowledgment.

"Hold on a second," she told her mom, lowering the phone from her ear.

"It might be a good idea to get out of town for the evening," he said. "If your mom wouldn't mind an extra guest, we can head that way now. Spend a few hours. If you want."

She squinted, unsure if seeing her mom was what she needed right now.

Austin bent forward at the waist. "I would love to meet your mama," he said, voice low. "Besides, I already showed you mine. You've got to show me yours."

One of his brothers snorted, and she smiled.

"I suppose fair's fair." She delivered the news to her mom, with one caveat. "Mom? Sounds like I can come, but I'm bringing a friend, and I'd be more comfortable if we had dinner at home, considering the circumstance."

"That's fine," her mom answered. "I'll get my carryout menus together and see what's for dinner."

Scarlet said her goodbyes and disconnected, then she stood.

"Looks like we're taking off," Austin announced.

"Yeah, yeah," Dean said, motioning him away with a teasing smile. "You take the pretty woman to dinner, and we'll stay here working."

Finn shook his head in feigned remorse.

Austin held her hand as they walked to his truck and opened her door. "Don't be afraid to let me know when you're ready to leave your mom's place. Even if we've barely arrived. Or if you need to lay down while we're there. I can entertain myself and your mother if necessary."

"You will definitely entertain my mother," she said dryly. She only hoped her mother wouldn't make an obvious show of her delight when she saw him. Handsome men were on the top of Trina's favorite things list. Having their undivided attention was another.

He smiled. "I'm just saying that I'm here to help, and you're not a bother. Sometimes I get the feeling you could use the reminder."

Scarlet nodded as she climbed inside and buckled up, deeply grateful fate had brought her to this man, and equally sad for the day they'd say goodbye.

Austin parked outside a grand two-story estate in the historic district of Trina Wills's town. He whistled appreciatively.

"Yeah," Scarlet agreed, looking up at the large Tudor-style home through the windshield. "I spent my teen years here. Mom got a good deal and worked hard to restore it."

"Just like you," he said.

"I picked up a thing or two from the project that made the work at my house a lot easier." She reached for the door handle and paused, as if steadying herself. "I've learned everything I know from her. The good and the bad."

Austin wanted to respond but didn't know how, so he climbed out and walked with her to the door. Scarlet rang the bell.

It only took a few moments for the large wooden barrier to swing open. An older version of Scarlet appeared before them with a smile. She wore dress pants and heels with a crimson blouse. Her fair hair was blown out and teased like a pageant woman, and her makeup was fully done.

"Baby," the older woman said, pulling her daughter into a hug. "I'm so glad you came. It's been too long. Come in. Come in." She motioned them into the two-story foyer. "Let me take your coats."

They removed their coats, and Mrs. Wills examined Scarlet. "Are you wearing pajamas?"

"No, Mom," she said. "This is Austin Beaumont, my—"

He stepped forward, offering his most respectable smile. "Nice to meet you, Mrs. Wills. I've heard so many nice things."

"Me too," she said. Her gaze traveled the length of him, appraising. She placed a stiff hand beside her mouth, as if to hide her next words. "You're right. He is handsome."

Scarlet's lids drifted momentarily shut. She reopened them with a resigned expression. "Dinner smells delicious."

Her mom cast another look in Austin's direction. "Call me Trina." Then she turned to lead them to a dining room table large enough for twelve. "I ordered Italian. Hope you like it."

Trina sat at the head of the long table, pushing salad around a plate while Austin and Scarlet each took a chair on either side of her and enjoyed two helpings of stuffed shells.

"How's Lydia doing with your clients while you're out?" Trina asked.

Scarlet paused, a forkful of pasta halfway to her mouth, and tension zinged in the air. "I haven't heard from her today."

Trina blinked. "You didn't call her? Have you at least checked in with the clients to see if they're happy with her level of service?"

"No." She returned her fork to the plate. "It's been a busy day."

"Every day is a busy one," her mom said. "Either that, or you aren't making the most of it. Am I right, Austin?"

He narrowed his eyes, certain he'd been snared in some sort of trap. "I'm not sure that's always the case," he said, unwilling to support her, but trying hard not to flat-out disagree. "Scarlet's right about our day. We've been on the move since breakfast. The only call she made time for was yours."

Trina stopped pretending to eat her salad and rested her hands on her middle. "My. I'd better stop before I need stretchy pants too."

Scarlet rolled her eyes, and Austin stifled a laugh. She changed the subject to her mom's workday, and things got lighter.

Trina obviously loved talking about herself, her sales and the new clients she'd be working with soon. She also mentioned a new boyfriend who thought she could stand to lose a couple of pounds and who was currently between jobs.

Scarlet's expression implied this was all par for the course with Trina.

Austin made a mental note to hug his mama a little tighter the next time he saw her. And to thank her for all the fussing she did to make his life nicer just because she could.

Despite the strange dynamic between mother and daughter, they seemed to enjoy their time together, more or less. And Trina boxed up the leftover food for them to take home.

She asked very little about what Scarlet was going through, and while he didn't understand that either, he was glad not to rehash it all. Scarlet seemed like she needed the break.

He drove home in the dark, Scarlet dozing beside him, and he couldn't help wondering what it would be like to have meals with Trina more often. And to see his family include Scarlet as well.

He was thankful for the peek inside her life, and he felt as if he understood her a little better now. Scarlet was the focused and giving one in their mother-daughter relationship, while Trina was the workaholic, driven by attention and supported at home by her child.

Regardless of their differences, it was clear they loved one another.

In hindsight, it made sense Trina hadn't asked more about the hell Scarlet was going through. The conversation would've steered too far away from her as the topic. And Scarlet had a lifetime of doing what she could to keep the spotlight on her mother.

A long practiced dance.

All the more reason Austin would work to make Scarlet the center of her world and his.

And he planned to tell her as much in the morning.

Chapter Twenty

Austin finished his third cup of coffee on the deck after breakfast. Scarlet sat beside him, still in her pajamas and bundled in the woven throw from the back of his couch. It was an image he wanted to see for years to come. And he'd promised himself he'd say so today. Which was the reason he planned to pour a fourth cup of coffee. He'd been up all night trying to decide how to broach the subject.

I know your life is in constant danger right now, emotions are high, you probably feel overwhelmed and confused about many things and my timing is terrible, but I'm falling in love with you. Let's discuss.

"You okay?" she asked, peering over her steamy mug. "You look stressed. Not that we don't have enough reasons for that. I've just never seen you actually look rattled until now. And we're here. Doing this." She extended an arm toward the mountains around them, the rocking chairs, the blue sky and the picturesque view of the creek rushing beneath. "So, what's up?"

He thought of a few reasonable ways to say he'd developed an attachment to her and didn't want to see it end, but none of them seemed right or worthy.

He'd become far more than attached.

"Lost in thought, I guess," he said, forcing a smile. "You?"

"A little," she said. "I've never thanked you for all this. For taking my case. For believing me when I came to you that day, when I wasn't even sure I believed myself. Then showing up and staying the course when everything went promptly to hell. You've catered and comforted. Now you're hosting me. It's a lot, and I was up half the night thinking I'm kind of awful for not saying this sooner."

The idea they'd both been awake last night but not together made him sad. He liked being with her and talking to her. They could've been happy instead of restless.

"Are you usually this involved in your cases?"

He frowned. She couldn't mean what he thought she meant. Could she? "No. Not like this."

He'd never once been attracted to a client. Never wanted to get to know them personally or have them in his life. He'd always done his best to help, nothing more.

There had just been something about Scarlet from the start. And the more he'd gotten to know her, the more he wanted to know. The more he wanted her to stay when this was over. Which was what he should be saying to her right now.

But the risk could outweigh the potential gain.

If Scarlet didn't feel the same way, there was a

chance she wouldn't be comfortable staying with him. He'd regret her absence in his home, but more importantly, he'd worry about her safety anywhere else. After what had happened at his office yesterday, he wasn't convinced the culprit wouldn't go to his family's farm for her. And the farm was the only other place he'd consider safe enough for anyone under constant threat of attack.

All reasons to wait until the criminal was captured and the danger gone before making an already complicated situation worse.

"So, your past girlfriends didn't get upset about your job because you'd started living with other women?"

He barked an unexpected laugh. "No. It's the time involved. Unless I'm on a stakeout, I always come home. Alone. But it's still a lot of long hours. Even after I get here, I work online, create files, paperwork, process contracts. I don't have a lot of time to go places. To date. I work, make time for my family and this place, then scrape together a little sliver of downtime when I can."

She set her coffee on the table at her side and turned to him, expression caught somewhere between contemplative and resolved. "I need to ask you something important, and I need you to answer me directly. Will you do that?"

He shifted, matching her position in the chair beside his. "If that's what you want." He swallowed and braced himself for what came next.

Her green eyes flickered away then back. "Yesterday, in the bathroom," she began. A blush spread across her face, pinking her cheeks, and her gaze dropped to his lips for one quick beat. "I thought you might've wanted to kiss me. I've spent the time since then wondering if I read everything wrong, or if something changed your mind. I stepped up and put my arms around your neck because I wanted you to kiss me, but if I misread you, I think I should apologize and let you know it won't happen again." She wrinkled her nose. "You've been so kind, and if I crossed a line or made you uncomfortable, I'm sorry."

His mouth opened to speak and his mind raced. He hadn't been able to make himself broach the subject, and she'd simply put it out there. No wonder he was falling for her. Scarlet was fearless. Unlike him, apparently. "I definitely wanted to kiss you in the bathroom yesterday."

Her eyes widened and her lips twitched. "Well, then I'm not sorry."

He smiled. "If I'm being fully honest, I've been thinking of kissing you a lot more often than I should."

She blushed, and his gaze dropped to her full pink lips.

He could practically taste them, almost feel them pressed to his. When his gaze returned to hers, she was watching him.

And like magnets, they both began to lean closer.

She laughed and pulled away when the distance between rocking chairs proved too much.

He stretched to his feet as Scarlet fell back into her chair, shaking her head at the temporary defeat. He offered his hand and pulled her up beside him, then wound an arm around her back. "We can't give up that easily."

"Agreed," she said. "We should try that again." The delight in her eyes thrilled him, and her contagious smile parted his lips as well.

Austin cradled her jaw in his palm, memorizing the lines of her face and absorbing this moment.

She closed her eyes and tipped her chin, then rose onto her toes.

The simple, openhearted gesture cracked something loose inside him, and he knew there wasn't any going back from there. He could only hope she'd feel the same when all was said and done.

And his phone rang.

Scarlet stepped away, brows raised. "Whoever's calling you right now is the absolute worst."

He laughed, dipping forward quickly and pressing a kiss against her temple before pulling the phone off the table at his side. "It's Finn."

She sighed, sobering a bit. "It's back to reality then."

He puzzled briefly at her meaning as he answered. "Hey, what's up?" Did she know being with her was the only reality he wanted?

Probably not because he'd yet to say so.

"I'm at the Coulter Realty office in town," Finn said. "Is Scarlet right there, or do you need to get her?"

"She's here."

Scarlet's brow furrowed.

"Hold on." Austin tapped his screen and lowered the phone between them. "All right. You're on speaker," he told his brother.

"Morning, Scarlet," Finn said, his voice oddly flat. "I'm at your office."

"More window paint?" she asked.

"No," Finn said. "A woman was attacked here this morning, and there's a threat at your desk. You two should probably get down here."

Fear flashed in Scarlet's eyes, and Austin's heart ached for her.

The stalker had crossed another line, bypassing destruction of property and trespassing. He'd attacked again, and this time it was someone Scarlet knew and likely cared for.

"What woman?" she asked, voice quaking.

"Lydia Stevens."

SCARLET BOUNCED DOWN the gravel lane on the seat in Austin's old truck then flew with him over paved country roads into town. Her heart raced and stomach lurched with flashbacks of her attack and fear for Lydia. Would she be hospitalized too? Would she be okay?

Did Lydia know Scarlet was the reason for her attack?

She was sure Austin would tell her this wasn't her fault, but he couldn't deny the truth. Scarlet's stalker wouldn't have been at the Coulter Realty office if not for Scarlet. He wouldn't have been so upset if she wasn't hiding out with Austin. And even if Scarlet wasn't sure what she could've done differently, Lydia's suffering was still directly linked to her. Scarlet should've predicted this somehow and protected her.

Austin covered her hand with his on the seat between them, gently stroking his thumb over her clenched fist.

"Did he say how badly she's hurt?" Scarlet asked. She'd barely heard anything Finn had said after Lydia's name.

"No. The paramedics were still working on her when he called."

Scarlet closed her eyes and sent up endless prayers for Lydia's well-being. For her stalker's capture and for no one else to be hurt this way.

The crowd outside her office was thick and deep, significantly larger than the group that had gathered outside the PI office the day before. The full gamut of emergency responders were there as well. An ambulance, a fire truck and three police cruisers crowded into the employee parking lot. Red and white lights flashed against the surrounding buildings on repeat, reflecting off the glass of nearby windows.

She and Austin jumped down from the truck and met at the hood, catching one another's hand then jogging the rest of the way to the building.

Uniformed officers had formed a barricade on the sidewalk. Thankfully, they recognized Austin and let them pass without question.

A moment later, he held the door so she could enter the office.

The space was full of people in uniforms. Cameras flashed and low voices murmured.

Time slipped beneath her, and the world seemed to tilt.

Lydia was laid out on a stretcher, eyes closed and

a padded collar around her neck. Dark bruises and fresh cuts peppered her jaw, forehead, eyes and nose.

Scarlet pressed her lips together, willing herself not to be sick on the office floor. And she hurried to the gurney's side. "Is she going to be okay?" she asked, clutching Lydia's hand.

Her friend's fingers didn't curl or grip back in response.

And Scarlet's tears began to fall.

The gurney inched forward as an EMT dislodged its brake. "I'm sorry," the man said, looking as if he meant it. "We'll do everything we can, but we have to go."

Scarlet pulled her hand away, and the paramedics guided an unconscious Lydia through the door.

Austin's arms curled around her, and she turned to bury her face against his chest. "We'll go to the hospital when we finish here, and I'll see if I can learn more."

"Thank you."

He stroked her hair, and she fought the urge to break down.

A sharp whistle cut through the air, and Scarlet forced herself upright, shoulders square and chin high.

Finn waved a hand overhead.

Austin pulled her against his side. "Time to see what he found."

The sea of uniformed personnel parted as they made their way down the aisle toward Scarlet's desk.

Finn stepped back, making room for her and Austin to take a look.

Her chair had been overturned and everything had been scribbled on. Her files, papers, the monitor. Even the fabric of her rolling chair and the desk itself. Two haunting words repeated again and again.

She's mine. She's mine. She's mine.

Chapter Twenty-One

Austin swore under his breath as Scarlet fell against his chest, breath rushing from her body. Even while doing all he could to protect her physically, the stalker was still getting in his jabs. Taking mental and emotional hits wherever he could.

"I can't believe this is happening," she whispered.

Austin wound his arms around her, gritting his teeth and pulling her in tight.

A storm of fury and heartbreak thundered inside him. Whoever was responsible for these attacks had clearly snapped. And wherever he was, he was a danger. The expressions on the medics' faces had made it clear that Lydia wasn't as lucky as Scarlet had been. Her injuries were more severe and would take far longer to heal. Though, she too would carry a lifetime of trauma from this man's hands.

The mere idea that Scarlet, who'd been strangled and left unconscious, was lucky compared to anyone was another sign of just how bad things had gotten.

Her fingers curled against his back as she clung to him. Her ragged breaths vibrated his chest and pierced his heart. Whatever thread of connection he'd imagined between them before had fast become a heavy rope. One he was sure could tow freight trains without a single tear.

"I've got you," he whispered, lowering his mouth to her ear. "Finn and the others are going to find the man who did this."

A camera flash straightened his spine. Behind her, a member of the crime scene unit documented evidence of the struggle.

Finn's and Dean's eyes were on Austin. They gave nods of understanding and acceptance before turning away. They saw what he'd yet to verbalize.

He was in love with Scarlet Wills.

"Come on," Austin said, sliding his hands onto her biceps. "Let's go to the hospital and see what we can find out."

Finn took a step in their direction as they broke their embrace. "I'll be there as soon as I can. We'll touch base then if you're still around."

Scarlet curled her arms around her middle, eyes haunted. "I want to stay at the hospital until I can see her," she said. "Her siblings are out of state now. I think I should wait with her mom until the rest of the family arrives. She shouldn't be alone."

Austin checked his watch. If they hurried, they'd arrive before his favorite volunteer headed home. "We'd better get moving." He guided Scarlet back to his truck and helped her inside. "You're very kind to think of Lydia's mother," he said. "She and Lydia will appreciate that."

"It seems like the least I can do." Scarlet's eyes were woeful as he closed the door.

He rounded the cab to the driver's side and climbed behind the wheel. "There's only one person to blame for any of this," he said softly. "And that person isn't you."

The drive to the hospital was silent, save for the sounds of Scarlet's unsteady breaths and tires on warped brick roads. He parked beneath the nearest streetlight just outside the visitors' lot and held her hand as they hurried inside.

Curious eyes turned briefly in their direction then away, not finding whoever or whatever they'd been seeking.

"What now?" Scarlet asked. "We're not family, so the staff won't talk to us. Do we wait for Finn to arrive?"

"We can, but it's a small town," he said, steering her toward a pair of chairs near the interior doors. "We won't have to wait long for information."

She offered a quizzical look, but sat.

"Do you know Mrs. Thatcher?" he asked.

"No. Does she work here?"

"She's a volunteer who makes those little knitted hats for newborns and fills in just about anywhere she can."

One of the paramedics from the real estate office moved into view before Scarlet could ask more questions.

Austin stood and offered his hand. "Were you able to get her stabilized?"

The other man nodded, expression grim. "She's undergoing tests, then they'll admit her for monitoring. She's stable, and that's something."

Scarlet rose. "Is she awake?"

"No, ma'am. Not yet." He opened his mouth to say something more, but his partner appeared behind him moving double time.

"We've got another call," she said. "One of the Briar kids fell from his horse."

The man gave a quick goodbye nod and hustled away.

Scarlet sighed. "Maybe I can steal a lab coat from the back of a chair and sneak around until I find her. It always works in sitcoms."

Austin fought a smile. "No need," he said, gaze locking on the woman he'd hoped to catch. "Here comes Mrs. Thatcher."

The older woman carried a large, quilted bag in one hand with an array of yarn strands hanging over the edge. Her white hair formed a crown on her head, and her milky blue eyes twinkled at the sight of him.

"Mrs. Thatcher," he said, lifting a wide smile. "How are you?"

She kissed his cheek and beamed. "Very well. Thank you. How's your mother?"

"Missing you," he said. "When will you get out to the ranch for lunch again?"

"Oh." She shrugged. "It's hard to say. I spend all my time knitting lately. This town has become a baby factory. There were four new little ones born since I arrived this morning." Her gaze slid to Scarlet. "All girls."

Scarlet offered a small smile.

"You remember Scarlet Wills," Austin prompted. "You were here when I got here on the evening she was attacked. You knew where I could find her."

The woman's eyes widened, and her gaze moved to Scarlet's throat. "I remember. Why are you back? Are you unwell?"

"I'm worried about my friend," Scarlet said. "The man who did this to me attacked another woman today. She was brought here a few minutes ago, and we're waiting to see her, if someone will allow it."

Mrs. Thatcher released a puff of air. "Oh, dear. You should sit."

Scarlet and Austin returned to their seats, and Mrs. Thatcher sat beside Scarlet. She took her hand and offered a cautious look in Austin's direction.

"Did you see her come through?" he asked.

"I might've," she said. "Would she have arrived in the last fifteen minutes?"

Austin nodded. "She was with the paramedics who left as you arrived just now."

Mrs. Thatcher's expression fell. "Then I know the one you mean. I thought she'd been in a car accident."

Austin shook his head.

The older woman turned her eyes to Scarlet, who was listening silently. "I'm so sorry."

"Mrs. Thatcher is the eyes and ears of this hospi- tal," he said. Even better, she was a shameless gossip, and a little flattery usually loosened her lips.

"My husband was the chief of surgery," she said proudly. "Rest his soul. He practically lived here, and so did I until our children were born, then again after

they'd grown. I know everything about this old girl."
She glanced around the room. "Always changing. Full
of life and tragedy."

"And the woman?" Austin asked. "Any chance you
know where we can find her?"

"I don't want her to be alone," Scarlet interjected.
"And I'd like to be with her mom when she arrives."

"They took her straight to the CT room for a scan,"
Mrs. Thatcher said. "The paramedics told the doctors
she'd had severe head trauma, was unconscious, and
they were concerned."

"How'd the scan look?" Scarlet asked.

"I don't know about that, but she's in the ICU now
for observation. You should go up to the third floor
waiting room. They keep fresh coffee and hot water
for tea. I'll bring something sweet when I come around
tomorrow."

"Thank you, Mrs. Thatcher," Austin said.

"Anytime, dear." She rose, and Austin did as well.
"Now, I'd better go see how the ladies at intake are
doing. Tell your mother I'll call soon."

"I will." He reached for Scarlet and pulled her up
with him. "This way."

HOURS SLOGGED BY in the little waiting room outside
the ICU. There wasn't anything to do and no real
reason to stay, but Scarlet insisted, so Austin did his
best to accommodate.

He requested a pillow and blanket from a volunteer to help Scarlet sleep more comfortably, and he'd

even begun to refill the waiting room coffee when it ran low or got cold.

Finn had come and gone with minimal news to share. Lydia's head scans had been clear, but she'd had significant neck trauma and was sedated to help with the pain. Her mother, who was local, had been visiting Lydia's brother in Texas. The family was flying in as soon as they could.

Yet another reason Scarlet wouldn't leave. She couldn't bear the thought of Lydia not having anyone waiting for her when she woke.

A guard had been positioned outside Lydia's room for due diligence. Just in case the attacker returned to silence her, if she'd seen his face.

The whole set of events had pushed Austin to his limits, and he'd spent a long while reviewing the evidence available while Scarlet slept. He'd seen his share of awful things, but he'd never seen them keep coming like this, and not at someone he loved.

He pulled the compact stun gun from his pocket and slid it into her jacket. She didn't want it, and he hoped she'd never have reason to use it, but knowing it was within her reach, even while she was safe beside him, offered a world of comfort. Only then, as the sunlight of a new day began to climb the windowsills, did Austin finally fall asleep.

SCARLET WOKE WITH a stiff back and aching neck. Her head pounded and her throat was dry. Austin was asleep in the chair beside her, long legs stretched out before him, while she and her pillow had leaned against his side.

A travel pack of pain pills sat on the table before them with a bottle of water.

She rubbed her eyes and rolled her shoulders, working out the kinks in her tender muscles, then opened the pain pills and water to take the medication.

The hospital bustled around her, and she was thankful for every hushed voice and hurried footfall. The halls had become eerie in the night, too quiet and still. Occasionally punctuated by a tragedy, racing crash team or other emergencies that left Scarlet on edge. Fearing Lydia had taken a turn for the worse and knowing no one would tell her if she had.

A trio of swiftly moving men appeared in the hallway, visible through the wall of waiting room windows. Her heart raced at the sight of a familiar face.

"Finn!" She clutched Austin's hand to wake him then creaked to her feet, wincing at the discomfort.

Austin stood instantly. "What happened? Are you okay?"

"Finn's here," she said, tracking the detective with her gaze. "And he's not alone. That means something, right?"

She moved into the hall as Finn and the officers approached.

"You're still here?" Finn asked, brows furrowed. He motioned the officers to continue on.

"I couldn't leave," Scarlet said. "Lydia's family isn't here yet." She glanced at the empty waiting room to be sure that was still true, and they hadn't arrived during the night.

His gaze shifted to his brother. "I'm on my way to see her now. Why don't y'all come back with me? It might soothe her to have a friend present when we talk. Officer Pratt is here to relieve Officer Grant of his shift, and Officer Meade will speak with the nurses."

Scarlet's heart swelled with hope. "Speak with her?"

"Yes. Lydia's awake."

Scarlet stifled the urge to hug him. She settled for following him into Lydia's room with Austin at her side.

Her friend's eyes opened and shut several times before opening to stay. "Scarlet?"

"Yes." Tears burst into existence as Scarlet hurried to Lydia's side. She clutched her right hand, avoiding the one with an IV, and did her best to remain calm and composed. "I'm here."

Lydia made a weak attempt to hold on to Scarlet's hand. "He came for me," she whispered, voice rough and raw.

"I know. I'm so sorry."

"Lydia?" Finn said. "I'm Detective Beaumont. I was assigned to Scarlet's case and I'll be working on yours as well. I promise I'm going to do everything in my power to apprehend the man who did this as soon as possible."

Lydia turned to watch and listen as he spoke. The wide red marks on her face from the day before were now swollen and black. A deep cut on her lip had been patched with a stitch, and there was blood on the white of one eye. A thick padded collar still circled her neck.

She released Scarlet's hand, brows furrowed and gaze distant, as if the reality of things was just filtering in. She lifted her fingers to the injuries on her face, and her expression crumbled.

"It's going to be okay," Scarlet said, voice quaking. "I'm here now and you're safe. No one will hurt you again. I promise. And I won't leave unless someone makes me. Even then I won't be far." She glanced to Austin, who'd made a similar promise to her once.

Finn pulled a little notepad from his pocket. "Were you able to get a look at the man who did this?"

She nodded then searched the ceiling with her eyes. "I think he was—" Her gaze snapped back to Scarlet. "He was looking for you. I said you weren't at work, and he said he knew that. He wanted to know where you were, but I didn't know. I said maybe at home."

"Can you describe him?" Finn asked again, rewording the question and working to regain her attention. "I know this is hard."

A sob broke on Lydia's lips and tears began to roll.

Her monitors beeped and a nurse came to check the situation. "Lydia? Morning, hon. Can you breathe for me? Nice and slow?" She frowned at Finn, then Austin, and slid her eyes over Scarlet. "This is an ICU. She's permitted to have one guest at a time, and all guests should be family. You know that, Detective."

"Her family is en route," he said. "Scarlet went

through something similar this week, and we hoped her presence would put Lydia at ease."

"How's that working?" she asked, gaze hard. "Wrap it up."

Austin raised his palms in innocence. "I'll step outside." He moved into the hall just beyond the door, outside Lydia's sight, but within Scarlet's view.

Lydia's lips quivered and her face contorted, fighting the tears. "He was tall with a beard. Not old. Not a kid either. I don't know. He wanted Scarlet. It was all he would say. Over and over. Where was she? Who was she with? Why was I lying?"

She sobbed.

Scarlet passed her a tissue. "I'm so sorry." The words were small and pathetic, but they were all she had to offer. The horror of the moment was too heavy to bear.

Lydia wiped her eyes, sucking in shallow, shuddered breaths.

Finn cast a cautious look at the nurse before trying again. He worked his jaw. "Was he familiar to you?"

"No." She shook her head and cringed, presumably at the pain. Her gaze flipped back to Scarlet. "But he knew me. He said my name."

"That's good information," Scarlet said, hoping to look calm and reassuring, while inside she cracked apart. "Detective Beaumont can use all of this to build a profile. To try to find him."

"Can you think of anything else?" Finn asked. "Even something small. A limp or lisp. A logo on his hoodie? A scar or tattoo?"

Lydia's eyes shifted, possibly sorting her thoughts

or searching her memories. Her monitors beeped more frequently.

The nurse's expression tightened. "Remember to breathe, sweetie. Last warning, Detective."

"He went to your desk," Lydia said. Her hand latched onto Scarlet's with unexpected fervor. "He left me on the floor and I watched—I watched him—"

"I saw," Scarlet said, covering her squeezing hand. "It's okay. We were at the office yesterday. Everything's been photographed."

"Photograph," Lydia repeated, gaze distant, as if recalling the moment.

"That's right. It's all being processed."

"No." A tear slid over her cheek. "He took your photograph."

"When?" Finn asked, voice harder than it had been since entering the room. "At the office party? Could he have been the photographer?"

Lydia shook her head again, skin paling and a sheen of sweat breaking across her brow.

"All right. That's enough." The nurse stretched her arms wide, as if to herd and push them from Lydia's room.

"No!" Lydia shoved onto her elbows. "He took the photograph from your desk."

The words hit Scarlet like an anvil as images from the day before returned. Everything had been covered in ink. Scribbled with that horrid message. *She's mine. She's mine.* Her desk had been overturned. Her papers scattered.

Austin stepped back inside, eyes darting from Scarlet to his brother. "Did you find a framed picture with her things?"

"No," Finn said, turning to Scarlet. "Why? What was in the photo?"

Her world came crashing down with the answer. "Me and my mother."

Chapter Twenty-Two

Scarlet dialed her mother for the thirtieth time as she and Austin raced along the highway between Marshal's Bluff and Holbrook. "Voice mail," she reported. "She's not answering her landline or cell phone. And no one at her office has seen her yet today."

"Hang in there," he said. "Finn's been in touch with her local police department, and they're looking for her too. All we can do is get there and help. Meanwhile, we have to keep trying."

"What if we don't find her?"

"We will," he said, reaching across the seat to grip her clasped hands, which were kneaded into a ball on her lap. "Can you think of anyone else she might've spoken with recently?"

Scarlet shook her head. Her mother didn't have friends. She had coworkers and clients, plus the occasional boyfriend. "I knew some of her coworkers before I moved, but there's a lot of turnover in this business. I don't know how many still work with her."

"If you know how to reach them, give it a try. Meanwhile, we'll stop at her home, then move to her office," he said. "We'll talk to neighbors and anyone else who might've seen her coming or going at either location. And we'll visit the local police department to introduce ourselves. Whoever is on this case will want to talk to you too."

Scarlet closed her eyes, combatting a swell of nausea and fatigue. Each time she was sure things couldn't get worse, they did. And this was far more horrible than anything she'd imagined.

This guy had her mother.

"He attacked Lydia yesterday," she said. "He's had enough time to drag my mom into another state and do anything he wants to her."

Austin gave her fingers a squeeze, and she braced for more words of false comfort that didn't come. "I know."

And those words were even worse.

Her mom's historic Tudor home appeared a while later, tucked neatly behind its brick fence. The limbs of mature trees swayed on the lawn, losing hordes of multicolored leaves with each bluster of the late fall wind.

Scarlet made a run for the front door. She rang the bell and knocked then peered through the windows, praying for signs of life inside. Hoping her mom would trundle into the foyer with a new man on her arm and a mimosa in one hand, having turned off her phone's ringer to embrace irresponsibility and new love.

"Car's gone," Austin said, hands cupped near his eyes as he peeked through the narrow garage windows.

"That's good," she said. "Right? I don't see any signs

of a struggle inside the home, so maybe she's just… out."

She wrapped icy arms around her middle, recognizing her words as a lie. The unseasonably cold day burrowed ice into her veins. Her mother wasn't out shopping or meeting someone for an early dinner. She wasn't with a new boyfriend. She was gone. Taken against her will.

"Do you have a key?" Austin asked. "We should check inside if we can."

Scarlet shook her head and glanced toward the home. "No." She hadn't had a key to her mom's place since the day she'd moved out and Trina had asked for it back. Scarlet tried the doorknob just in case. "Locked."

"All right." Austin moved toward the waiting truck. "We'll check her office next."

The drive into town was short. A cruiser sat in the parking lot when they arrived.

"Why do you think the cops are here?" Scarlet asked, climbing down from the truck and hoping she didn't already know. Her teeth began to chatter as her exhausted body flooded with adrenaline she had no way to process.

The last time they'd arrived at an office like this with a police presence, they'd found Lydia beaten and unconscious.

"This is routine," Austin said, matching his stride to hers across the parking lot. "No flashers. No other first responders. My best guess is that these officers are just following up like Finn requested."

She exhaled, shaking her hands out hard at the wrists. "Okay. That makes sense."

"I always make sense," Austin said, drawing her eyes to his.

A small smile tugged her lips.

"I've got you," he told her, swinging open the glass office door and waiting for her to pass. "Whatever comes, we'll face it together."

Her heart swelled, and her lips quivered. "Thank you."

Unlike the more modern satellite location in Marshal's Bluff, her mom's office was set in a historic brick building with a row of curtained windows and tidy flower beds along a stone walkway.

The homey theme carried through to the interior. Each agent had a large wooden desk on a colorful rug with two armchairs positioned before it and a matching chair on wheels behind it. A refreshments area with coffee, tea and a minifridge for bottled water and juices anchored a wall near the restrooms. Vases with fall-colored blooms sat on side tables with framed photos of top-selling agents and printed lists of company attributes.

"This is cozy," Austin said, pausing in the entryway to look around.

"Each office is designed to be most attractive to the clientele in that area," Scarlet said. "It's all about the outdoor views in our town. People move there to enjoy the seaside."

The Marshal's Bluff office was utilitarian, mostly glass and metal, meant for brief visits on a client's way back outside. The interior was pale blue and the art featured boats, gulls and images of the sea. No one wanted to be indoors in Marshal's Bluff. Whereas Holbrook was all about history and hospitality.

A uniformed officer spoke to a woman at a desk near the back. "And this is her calendar?" he asked.

"Yes. We keep our own schedules. Trina's is always full. We don't see a lot of her, unless it's a paperwork day and she's here playing catch-up." The woman's gaze jumped to Scarlet and Austin as they stepped forward. She gasped. "Oh, my stars, I thought you were her."

The stern-faced officer looked their way. His pale blue eyes were creased at the corners and tight with concern. He was older than Scarlet, probably older than her mother, but fit with an air of authority that gave Scarlet hope. "I'm afraid this isn't a good time," he said. "Can Ms. Reese take your name and number and give you a call in a bit?"

"No." Scarlet moved in their direction. "I'm Scarlet Wills. This is Austin Beaumont. My mother's Trina Wills."

The man's expression morphed from politely patient to apologetic. "I'm sorry. Come on in. I'm Officer Barrow and this is Cindy Reese, a coworker of your mother's."

"Please sit," Cindy said, pointing to a seat at the desk beside hers. Her white sweater set and long, shapeless blue skirt reminded Scarlet of her elementary school librarian. Her gray bun and pencil tucked through the knot finished the look perfectly. "That's your mama's desk," Cindy said. "You look just like her. Anyone ever told you?"

Scarlet tried to smile. "It's been a while, but I used to hear it all the time." She lowered herself into the seat and covered her mouth at the sight of her mother's things. All neat as a pin. All untouched, waiting for her return. And the same framed photo that Scarlet kept on her desk stood beside her mother's monitor as well. "Austin," she whispered. "Look."

He placed his hands on her shoulders, and she did her best to soak up his strength.

Scarlet ran a fingertip over the glass, tracing her mother's cheek.

The large paper calendar beneath her opposite hand was lined in client names, addresses and times. The color-coded system had been in use for her mother long before the realty company they worked for had a website and apps to organize an agent's schedule.

"It looks as if your mother had an appointment on the books for first thing this morning," the officer said, drawing Scarlet's eyes to the paper calendar. "I'm guessing she went straight to the home on Elm after leaving her place. We've tried the number for the client, but no one answered." He pointed to the digits written with the name and address where her mother planned to meet a client at 9:00 a.m.

Austin set his hands on his hips. "He's been using disposable phones for related crimes in Marshal's Bluff."

Officer Barrow grunted, clearly unimpressed but unsurprised. "Detective Beaumont gave me a pretty solid rundown," he told Austin before returning his gaze to Scarlet. "I'm very sorry for what you're going through. My team and I are working in tandem with the Marshal's Bluff police force, and we'll do everything we can to locate your mother and make sure she's safe."

"Thank you," Austin said.

Scarlet nodded, throat tight.

The desk phone rang, and the room stilled. Air thickened around her shoulders as she stared at the screen.

"That's the number I called earlier," Officer Barrow said. "From the morning appointment. Let's see if your mother arrived as planned." He leaned forward, arm outstretched, as if intending to answer the call.

Scarlet lifted a hand to block him. Her gaze swept the caller ID screen then the paper calendar under her hand. And a sense of foreboding curled around her spine. She pressed the speaker button on the phone. "Coulter Realty," she said warily. "Scarlet speaking."

"Hello, darling," a low voice seethed. "I knew you'd answer my call."

Austin was at her side in the next moment, his cell phone poised before the speaker, a recording app already in use.

Scarlet gripped his arm then pushed on. "You did?"

"I know everything about you. And I see you right now," he said. "Still with that man. Still unwilling to listen."

"Is my mom with you?" Scarlet asked, ignoring his menace. "Can I talk to her?"

"Not while you're keeping him around."

"What if I ask him to go outside?" she asked, cringing slightly at the thought.

"Tell him you're mine!" he roared, voice vibrating the little speaker and sending Scarlet's hammering heart into her throat.

She reeled back, feeling as if she'd been slapped and remembering women got hurt when he got angry. "I'm sorry," she said, rising to lean over the phone and beg. "I'm so sorry. Please don't be mad at my mom. I didn't mean to upset you. It's not her fault. I'll do better."

"You will," he said, voice lower and assured. "Because infidelity has a price."

The line went silent, and Scarlet's world collapsed around her.

Chapter Twenty-Three

Austin sent the audio recording to Finn, then he turned his focus to Scarlet, who looked as if she was in shock.

Officer Barrow had cracked immediately into action, voice rumbling through the quiet office as he recounted the details to Finn and his team. The front door quickly opened and closed as he moved outside.

Cindy Reese stared after him. "Where's he going?"

"Looking for the caller, I imagine," Austin said. "Are you okay?"

She nodded woodenly then cast her attention to Scarlet, staring and motionless, before heading to the refreshments table. "I'll find something for her to drink. I think she's in shock. Heaven knows I can't blame her."

"Thank you."

"I'm not in shock," Scarlet whispered, still staring blankly ahead.

Austin crouched at her side. "Are you sure?"

Her chest rose and fell in steady breaths. The hairs on her arms stood at attention, bolstered by a cascade of goose bumps.

"Scarlet?"

Cindy returned with a steaming mug and a half-sized bottle of water. "I wasn't sure you liked tea, so I brought water too," she said, setting both on the desk.

Scarlet didn't move or respond.

"Is she okay?" Cindy whispered. "Should she see a doctor?"

"I'm thinking," Scarlet said.

"Oh." Cindy set a packet of crackers beside the water and backed up. "That's good. I'll leave you to it."

Austin raised his palm in thanks as the older woman turned away.

"Do you think he's still out there?" Scarlet asked. "Parked across the street or lurking on the corner?"

"I'm sure he's already moved on," Austin said. Leaving them to chase their tails as usual.

"He knew I was here. Sitting at her desk. Knew I'd answer the phone. How?"

Austin looked at the windows, each with a slatted wooden miniblind and sheer curtains parted at the center. "I don't know. He likely guessed."

"After following us here," she said. "Knowing I'd look for my mother."

"That, or he saw my truck in the lot. From there he could've assumed you were at her desk. Just because he said he saw you, doesn't mean he did. And there's a chance he was speaking figuratively when he said he saw you. As if he knows you, not that you were literally in view." Though even Austin had trouble believing that theory. Whoever this guy was, he'd been clinging to Scarlet like a second skin from day one. And he'd yet to figure out how he was doing it.

And now he had her mother.

The door opened again, and Officer Barrow strode back inside, cell phone no longer at his ear. "There weren't any signs of the caller on the street, but he could've easily walked or driven away. A team's been dispatched to review local security footage in search of a car matching the description provided by Detective Beaumont. For now, it's probably best that Ms. Wills find someplace safe to stay out of sight."

Austin nodded, his mind already working through their prospects. His place was the safest, but it was back in Marshal's Bluff, and he knew better than to ask Scarlet to leave this town, where her mother had gone missing. She'd want to stay close to the places and things in her mother's world. There were a handful of inns on the way into town, but those wouldn't be any easier to guard than any other house, which only left hotels. Something outside Holbrook, but not as far as home, would be best. Some place within a ten- to fifteen-minute drive, in case they were needed in a hurry.

Scarlet tugged on his coat sleeve, gaze still fixed on the paper calendar under hand. "Look."

Officer Barrow moved to his side. "What is it?"

One slender finger touched a set of initials at the top of Trina Wills's schedule for the prior day. TS.

Austin examined the script, then looked to her for explanation. The letters were written near the date without indication of time or purpose. "What does it mean?"

Scarlet turned bewildered green eyes to him. "Tech Services."

His mental wheels spun as the pieces of the puzzle began to fall into place.

Cindy returned, an expectant look on her brow. "Trina has been having issues with her company laptop and accounts. Maybe she scheduled a meeting to sort it out."

Scarlet paled. She'd had her share of similar problems not long ago. "What if the person who left the image of me from the party didn't actually attend the party or take the picture?" she asked. "What if he had access to the photos from that night because he was the one selecting which ones to use?"

Austin recalled the Coulter Realty website, where images from events like the one in question were featured on the About page.

"Tech Services would've been given all the images, so they could upload a few to the site."

Austin's fingers curled. The culprit had been in Scarlet's life all along. Tucked neatly into the background.

"I'll call Detective Beaumont," Officer Barrow announced.

Scarlet moved her cell phone onto the desk and navigated to Coulter Realty's corporate page, then to the staff directory.

"Smart," Austin said, crouching for a clearer view over her shoulder.

"Tech Services," she said, zooming in on a candid shot of the men and women who made up the department. "I talked to someone from TS almost every day during the transition to the new website. Something was always going wrong or haywire with my new email or the password. I must've had it reset a half dozen times. Then I needed help with the contact form when I began to receive showing requests. They were assigned to me, but I didn't always get a notification in time to make the appointments. It was a long process filled with hiccups. But what if they weren't all hiccups?"

"Who did you talk to?" he asked. "You said you spoke to someone every day. Was it always the same person?"

"Yes," she said, the word barely a whisper. "Him."

Her hand trembled violently as she passed the phone to Austin, nearly dropping it in the process. She'd zoomed in on one man in a group of smiling, carefree faces around a table. Sandy hair. Dark eyes. A narrow face and build. "Greg. I've never met him in person or seen him before now." An ugly sound ripped from her core. "That's the man who attacked me."

Austin returned the image to normal size, temper raging silently beneath his surface. The man who'd attacked two women, threatened, stalked and now abducted someone looked just like everyone else in the photo. A perfect wolf in sheep's clothing.

He wrapped Scarlet in a hug.

"Tech Services," Officer Barrow said, back on his

cell phone nearby. "I need the contact information on a man called Greg."

A tremor spread through Scarlet as they listened to the seasoned officer command someone at Coulter's corporate location.

"That's the one." His gaze flickered to Scarlet then Austin. "Greg Marten."

Austin held his eye contact, jaw locked, and a silent understanding passed between them. Greg Marten's reign of terror was ending now.

"I need Marten's contact information and everything you know about him. I'd also like to speak with the other members of his department... He's a person of interest in several ongoing investigations with both the Holbrook and Marshal's Bluff police..." Barrow rubbed his forehead, apparently unhappy with the response he received. "Then I'll be there with a warrant inside the hour." He disconnected the call and made another while heading for the door. "Get her somewhere safe while I run this guy down," he told Austin, before pulling his attention back to the phone. "This is Barrow. I need to speak to someone in Judge Touran's office." He raised a hand in good-bye and strode back into the day.

Scarlet stood, gripping Austin's elbow for balance. "Greg tampered with my account and had access to my schedule. That's why he always knew where I would be. He could've even watched me through my laptop camera. It was company-issued after all. So was my phone. And I'll bet he's the reason your security cameras weren't working when your office windows were vandalized."

"We've got his name now. Finn will know everything else about him soon. Let's go somewhere and lay low."

"I don't want to leave town until my mom is found."

"I know," he said. "I have an idea."

SCARLET FOLLOWED AUSTIN into the lobby of an upscale boutique hotel on the edge of town. The building was grand, with a crimson awning, doorman and the year 1912 carved into a stone beside double-glass doors.

The parking lot had been relatively full considering it wasn't tourist season, and they didn't seem to be near anything of significant importance. But she supposed staying here was a treat any time of year.

The arching foyer was inlaid with golden accents and a mural of the sky. Crimson carpet ran underfoot, outlined in large marble squares. An ornate round table centered the space, topped with a massive floral arrangement that had probably required two people to carry it.

A man in a suit stood ready at the desk beyond. "Welcome to The Carolina Grand. How can I help you?"

"Hello," Austin said. "We'd like a room."

"You're in luck," he said, without referencing the computer screen at his side. "We have one left."

Men and women crisscrossed the space around them in bunches, all clearly delighted. Their voices and laughter echoed off the high ceiling, walls and floor.

Austin frowned at the busyness. "Is there something going on?" he asked. "A convention?"

"A weekend wedding," the man said. "If you're looking for peace and quiet, it might not be the right place for you. But, if you're fans of music, there'll be a live quartet at meal times in the house restaurant and a local band in the bar, which could make for fun evenings."

Austin grinded his teeth in consideration, keen eyes scanning the exits and doorways. "Where is the available room located? Which floor?"

"First."

His frown deepened, and he glanced at Scarlet.

The man behind the counter furrowed his brow. "Is that all right?"

"Maybe," Austin said. "Does your restaurant have a private entrance?"

"No. All guests use the main doors. Why?"

"What about the bar and kitchen?" Austin asked. "How many entrances are on this floor?"

The other man reared back his head and looked to Scarlet. This time, a bit concerned.

"I'm okay," she said, offering a small smile. "He's just incredibly diligent."

The man's attempt to match her smile failed.

"How many entrances in total?" Austin repeated.

"Four. One on each face of the building. North. South. East. West." He moved his hand from wall to wall, as if the exits were visible from where they stood.

"And on which side is the room located?"

He pointed again. "The Thurston Suite is east facing and well equipped. Anything you don't find there can be delivered to you from our pantry or closet, and our concierge is full-service. Anything you need, he can acquire."

"I doubt that," Austin muttered.

The man leaned forward, looking pointedly near their feet. "Do you have any luggage?"

"No."

Scarlet sighed at the ridiculousness of the conversation, and how utterly bizarre they must look and sound to this man. Eager to take the last available room, but worried about the building's entry points, and all the while without a single duffel bag or suitcase between them.

"We didn't expect to stay in town when we arrived," she said. "But circumstances have changed."

"And you want the room?"

"Yes," Austin answered. "And I'll need to speak to your manager."

The desk clerk took his time checking them in, probably wishing he'd told them the hotel was full. Then, Austin spoke briefly with the shift manager, delivering the details of their situation. He promised to pass the information on to the hotel manager when her shift began.

The walk to their room was long and slightly convoluted in the historic building. They turned left twice before finding the hallway with the last available suite. They were each given a key card to access the door, though she had no intention of going anywhere without Austin. And he let them inside with a swipe.

The space was small, as promised—a large four-post bed at the center took the lion's share of space. An armchair in the corner shared a stand with the bed. A table with two chairs stood before a window at the far wall, and a restroom was just inside the door from the hallway. Plush blue carpet covered the floor, and large oil portraits in gilded frames adorned the walls. A minifridge and small television were the only signs of the millennium.

In another life, in a room like this with a man like Austin Beaumont, she'd never have time to turn the television on. But in that life, her mother wouldn't be in the violent hands of a deluded, dangerous man.

Chapter Twenty-Four

Scarlet showered and slipped into a T-shirt and underthings they'd ordered after settling in.

Austin had arranged for anything not provided in
the room, like clothing, to be picked up from a local
store by the hotel concierge, who really did handle everything. He'd also ordered a tray of soups and breads
from the restaurant for their dinner, and he hadn't forgotten her glass of red wine.

He'd met her every need without being asked, and
though Scarlet's world was crumbling, she felt utterly
cared for. A new sensation she never wanted to let go
of. In fact, she hoped to do the same for him someday.

Austin rose from his chair at the table when she
stepped away from the steamy bathroom in her big
T-shirt and fuzzy socks. Damp hair hung loose over
her shoulders, and she shivered, suddenly regretting
not wrapping herself in the cushy terry cloth robe.

"It's all yours," she said, hoping to look less self-
conscious than she felt and moving to one side of the
bed to peel back the covers.

A new show had started on the television, which had

been playing softly for hours since their arrival. They'd watched a marathon of sitcoms from her childhood while intermittently eating and touching base with Finn for new information. He never had much to offer, but he and Officer Barrow were exhausting even the tiniest leads, which made a terrible situation slightly better.

The last update had come more than two hours before, and all that was left for her to do now was wait. She wasn't sure she'd be able to rest well, but it was late and sleeping was the fastest way to pass the time until he called again.

"Thanks." He gathered his things and headed for the bathroom, which was still seeping steam.

The closet door was ajar in the corner, and a stack of folded blankets sat on the armchair, topped with a pillow. Somehow, the time they'd spent collecting updates on the search for her mother and watching television had distracted her from the implications of sharing a room with one bed. She'd felt comfortable and safe, despite the overarching circumstances, just as she had in the days shared at her home and his.

Now thoughts of their sleeping arrangements were front and center in jarring and slightly thrilling ways. She couldn't ask him to sleep in a chair while she had a queen-size bed to herself. That was just bad manners. And impractical.

She dragged her attention to the bathroom, where a shower had started running, then made up her mind. She put the pillow and blankets away, closed the closet door and slid into bed as planned.

Every splash of water in the next room brought an

image with it that she couldn't ignore. Memories of his arms curved gently, protectively around her. His hands on her skin offering comfort. His breath on her lips when they'd nearly kissed.

She squirmed beneath the cool cotton sheets, restless for something she didn't want to name.

When the bathroom door opened again, Austin appeared in pajama pants and bare feet. His hair was wet and a T-shirt clung to the damp planes of his chest.

Scarlet felt a rush of heat from the crown of her head to her toes.

He stared at the empty chair then turned his eyes to her. "You put the blankets away?"

She nodded and pulled the comforter back. "I think we should share the bed. It doesn't make any sense for you to sit in a chair all night. Given the days we've had lately, we both need some rest, and you won't get it there." She nodded to the place where his blanket stack had been. "We need to be ready for whatever the morning brings."

Austin released a breath. "You're not wrong there." He dropped the pile of clothes he'd worn all day onto the table then climbed into bed beside Scarlet and turned out the light. A moment later, he rolled over and leveled his face with hers.

The soft glow from the television flickered in the darkness.

"On or off?" he asked, raising the remote he'd grabbed from his nightstand.

"Off."

Her eyes adjusted quickly to the darkness, and she

smiled at him lying so close to her. "Do you think we'll hear any more from Finn tonight?"

"It's possible," he said.

Finn and his team were working every angle. Interviewing Greg's friends, family and coworkers. Looking for properties he or his family might own that went unused this time of year, like a cabin or lake house. Checking the vehicle databases for anything he could be driving, including boats he could use to hole up on the water. On top of that, Tech Services had spent the day digging into his work computer, and Marshal's Bluff officers had combed his home.

"It's just a matter of time now," Austin said.

She nodded, liking the way that sounded. "It seems impossible for him to hide."

"I think it is," Austin said confidently. "It would be hard enough for someone in their right mind to stay out of Finn's grasp for long. Add in the fact that Greg's juggling some kind of mental break, and he's got your mom in tow, and I don't think he'll last another twenty-four hours. I suspect they'll close in soon. He'll know he's caught and be forced to leave Trina behind to make a break for it."

Scarlet raised a hand to wipe a renegade tear. "I hope you're right. I hope he won't hurt her before he leaves her." At least no more than he'd likely hurt her already, forcing her into his control.

"Hey." Austin brushed hair away from her face with the backs of his fingers. "You okay?"

"My emotions are everywhere, but I'm fine. It's a lot to think about, and it's been a long week."

"All the more reason to rest." He tucked the lock of hair behind her ear then stroked his palm over her shoulder and down her arm.

Heat from his touch sizzled a path across her skin, and she shivered.

Austin pulled back, but she caught his fingers and rested their joined hands on the blankets between them.

Their eyes locked and breaths mingled in the darkness. Electricity charged the air.

"Are you still thinking about kissing me?" Scarlet asked, releasing his hand. "Because I'm thinking of kissing you." She slid her fingers along the curve of his neck then stroked his jaw with her thumb.

He stilled beneath her touch, and his Adam's apple bobbed. "I am."

"And?" she asked, somehow closer to him than she'd been a moment before.

He crooked one arm beneath the pillow supporting his head and let his free hand trail the curve of her hip. Then he pressed against the small of her back, eviscerating the little space left between them. Austin's lips curved into a small, mischievous grin as he pressed his mouth gently to hers.

Scarlet's body melted against him. She'd never wanted to be kissed by any man so much in her life. And unlike so many people liked to say, the anticipation was not better than the reality. It was as if his mouth was made for hers, and every fiber of her ignited at his touch. The soft moan that escaped her drew a full smile across his lips.

He pulled back and stared, heat and longing in his eyes. His heart hammered beneath her palm on his muscled chest. "I won't ever let anyone hurt you again," he vowed, voice low and thick with truth. "And I don't want to leave you when this man is caught. I'm hoping you'll ask me to stay."

Emotions rose and bloomed in her as she kissed him in response. His perfect words filled her, because she didn't want him to go. She found the hem of his shirt and tugged until he pulled it over his head and tossed it onto the floor. She removed her shirt as well.

Austin cussed at the sight of her bare breasts. He cupped them reverently in his hands as he kissed her once more.

When her head was light and her body boneless, he moved his skilled tongue along the plane between her breasts. She gasped as he stroked and suckled one taut nipple, angling his body more firmly against hers.

Her hands fisted in his outgrown hair and his mouth drifted lower. "Austin."

"Still okay?" he asked, as he continued to explore.

She arched in answer and invitation.

"Yes?" he asked between kisses, working a magic rhythm with his touch.

"Yes."

He dragged his lips up the column of her throat.

The gentle slide of his tongue on her skin sent shock waves of pleasure through her limbs. She rocked her hips with every pulse of his hand. Austin's kisses were devouring and he swallowed her needy moans. She wanted nothing more than to be consumed by every inch of him.

She gripped the waistband of his pajama pants, desperate to feel more of his bare skin on hers.

"Scarlet?" he whispered, as her body tipped toward the brink of unraveling. "Are you sure this is what you want?"

"You are the only thing I want," she said, and his eyes flashed hot with pleasure.

Then he brought her swiftly over the edge.

Austin woke the next morning with Scarlet's hand in his. Her lithe body curled against his side. He stroked the hair from her cheek, pressed a gentle kiss to her forehead and hoped like hell she'd want him today the way she had last night. Because there wasn't anything he wanted more than her, and he didn't see a future where that would change.

He longed to kiss her awake and love her once more, before the busyness of their day began. More than that, he needed to reiterate his feelings and intentions so there'd be no questions or misunderstandings by the light of day. His heart was hers for the taking.

A shrill ring interrupted his thoughts, turning his eyes to the phone on his nightstand.

He grabbed the receiver quickly, silencing the sound, but his shifting body roused Scarlet anyway.

"Who is it?" she asked.

"I don't know." He pulled the phone to his ear. "Hello?"

"Mr. Beaumont?" a strained male voice asked.

"Yes." He slid upright against the headboard, senses on sudden alert. "Who's this?"

"This is the hotel manager," the voice continued. "There's a man in the lobby looking for the woman you arrived with yesterday. He has her photo and is claiming that she's his wife and she's been abducted. He's making quite a scene."

"What does he look like?"

"Sandy hair, brown eyes. He's wearing jeans and a hooded sweatshirt."

Adrenaline surged in Austin's body as he swung out of bed and began to dress on autopilot. "Where is he now?"

"In the lobby. He's arguing with the desk clerk who's refusing to give any information. I sneaked into my office to call you."

"Good work. I'm on my way. Call the local authorities and tell them what you've just told me." Austin returned the receiver to its cradle and swiped his cell phone off the nightstand.

Scarlet sat, clutching blankets to her chest. "What's going on?"

"Greg's in the lobby trying to find out which room we're in. The hotel manager is calling local authorities, and I'm going out there to see if I can get my hands on him before he gets away." Austin tucked a pair of handcuffs into his pocket and grabbed his wallet and key card. "Get dressed and be ready when I come back. Don't answer the door for anyone."

She nodded, already scrambling for the bathroom. "Be careful."

Scarlet was in turbo mode. She dressed in seconds and headed back into the main room, preparing to stuff their things into bags in case they needed to leave in a rush.

The door clicked again, stilling her in her tracks. Austin had barely been gone a minute. What had he forgotten? Or had something big already gone wrong?

She pulled on her coat as she hurried to meet him. "Everything okay?"

A familiar figure moved into view as she rounded the corner.

Greg Marten glared, wild eyed, and raised the gun in his hand.

Chapter Twenty-Five

"This way," Greg said with a flick of his wrist, pointing to the door with his gun.

Scarlet held her ground, mind racing. If he shot her, everyone would hear and she might live. If she went with him, her odds of survival would be infinitely thinner. What she needed to do was stall. Austin would be back soon. "How did you get in here?"

"Key card." He grinned. "They're not hard to copy if you know what you're doing and can get close enough to the one you want. I know what I'm doing, and it's surprising how careless the housekeeping staff is these days."

She struggled to swallow. The harmless guy from Tech Services had somehow become the ultimate modern-day villain. "The manager is on to you," she said. "He called the police. You'd be smarter to run now than to add another crime to your spree." If he valued being clever, maybe he'd take her advice and go.

Greg grimaced and marched forward, extending his gun in her direction until her eyes closed. "I am very smart." A hand clamped over her wrist, and he jerked her hard, nearly knocking her off her feet. "Don't give me any trouble, or I will leave without you, and I'll kill your mother as punishment."

Scarlet's ears rang, and her thoughts clouded. Everything dissipated from her mind except her mother. And she let Greg tow her into the hall.

"No one's coming to save you this time," he said, guiding her along with a stern hand. "A bunch of hotel guests are in the restaurant making a ton of noise, and your PI is chasing his tail in the lobby. I've got you all to myself. Now, out you go." He shoved her through an exit door, into a small lot where a large truck was making a delivery.

She scanned the traffic-packed streets nearby and winced at the sight of the old navy sedan local police had been searching for.

Greg opened the passenger door. "Get in and climb over. You're driving."

"What?"

He pushed her across the armrests and into the driver's seat then planted the keys on her lap. His hand lingered unnecessarily. "Drive. Make a left onto Main Street and hurry, or we'll be too late to save your mother."

Terror seized her lungs as she dug the key from beneath his palm and started the car. She glanced through the window as she shifted into gear, wishing for Austin to burst from the hotel and save her.

"Do you hear any sirens?" Greg asked, turning her attention to his smug face.

She blinked away the tears forming in her eyes. "No."

"That's because I'm the one who called your room, not a manager. I'm the one who drew your PI away. No one called the cops. There's no help on the way. Right now, your friend is standing around wondering what happened. He'll probably demand to speak to the manager who will have no idea what he's talking about. I've outmaneuvered all of them. Now you and I can start the life we're meant to have."

Austin raced down the hallway, past a housekeeping cart. The staffer's lanyard hung from one side. He considered stopping for a fleeting moment, to tell her not to disturb his room, not to frighten Scarlet who was already terrified and alone, but he couldn't spare the time. Not if Greg Marten was in the lobby and local police were on their way. This was Austin's time to take down their enemy and see that he was cuffed and charged.

The hotel restaurant was packed as he jogged over the crimson carpet to the desk. Guests spilled from the open French doors, bringing a cacophony of voices, laughter and music along with them. Greg could blend easily into the rambunctious morning crowd and vanish through a side door if Austin didn't hurry.

"Where did he go?" Austin called, erasing the final few yards to the welcome desk.

The young man behind the counter blinked. "Who?"

"The man who was here looking for his wife. Your manager called me. I'm Austin Beaumont." He dug his wallet and PI license from one pocket and flashed it across the counter.

The man frowned. "I don't know anything about that, sir."

"Who was working here a minute ago? I need to talk to them. No." He waved a panicked hand, feeling the world tilt beneath him. "I need to speak to your manager."

"Can I help you?" A regal-looking blonde woman in a black pantsuit and heels strode confidently from a nearby doorway. "I'm the hotel manager, Eva Branson."

Austin stilled then stumbled back, realization gripping his heart and chest like a vise. The hotel manager he'd spoken to only minutes before had been a man. "Call the police," he demanded. "Tell them Austin Beaumont said to get here. Now!"

He tore back through the cavernous lobby, down the hallway and past the housekeeping cart to his room. He pressed the key card to the door and swung it open, his heart and final thread of hope in the balance.

But as expected, the room was empty.

"WHERE IS MY MOTHER?" Scarlet asked, fingers aching from her grip on the wheel, fear stiffening her posture.

The old sedan smelled of motor oil and cigarette smoke. Both scents likely permeated the fabric seats long before Greg made the purchase. A pair of orange tree-shaped air fresheners dangled from the rearview mirror on white springy cords. The back seat was empty, the car otherwise immaculate.

"Turn right," he said, ignoring her question and pointing to the upcoming highway entrance. "Get on the interstate, then stay in the left lane and keep up with traffic until I say otherwise."

She looked at the car beside her, wishing the other driver would make eye contact and see her distress. The young man behind the wheel of the SUV sang along to the radio, oblivious to her terror. She changed lanes, losing hope, and something thumped softly in the trunk.

"Good," Greg said, satisfied she was cooperating.

Her heart sank. Getting on the highway would mean disappearing, maybe permanently. Somewhere Austin and local law enforcement would never find her.

A flash of red and white in her side-view mirror caught her eyes. Austin's old truck appeared, cutting in and out of traffic with ease.

"Use your signal," Greg said. "Make the turn."

She shot him a venomous look and eased her foot off the gas pedal. Surely he wouldn't kill her while she was driving. "First tell me where my mother is!"

The muted thumping she'd heard earlier grew louder and more fervent. Scarlet jerked her head around to face the back seat, earning her a honk as she swerved.

"Is someone in the trunk?" Scarlet gasped. "Is that my mom?"

Greg pressed the gun's barrel to her ribs. "She's fine. Now pay attention and drive. Getting into a car accident won't be good for her."

Scarlet bit her lip, eyes darting to Austin's truck in her rearview mirror. He was a block away but gain-ing on them. She slowed, poking along, allowing cars to pass her.

"What are you doing?" Greg demanded. "Drive faster!"

"I'm nervous," she snapped. "I don't like traffic or having guns pointed at me. I think you locked my mom in the trunk. How am I supposed to handle this? Why did you even take her? Do you want me to hate you?"

"I want you to do what I say. She's your motivation," he said. "Mommy stays safe as long as you obey and stop seeing that man. She's in the trunk so you stay calm and don't try anything ridiculous while you're behind the wheel."

Scarlet's mouth opened then shut. She could be angry, and she could be mean. But her mom would be the one he punished, and she couldn't allow that.

"Get on the highway."

She checked the rearview again. Austin had moved ahead by another car length, but the traffic light was yellow. He wouldn't make it through the intersection with her.

Greg pointed the gun into the back seat then cocked it. "Run the light or a bullet goes into the trunk."

Scarlet released a defeated sob as she jammed the gas, launching them onto the highway.

Austin pounded his hand against the horn as the sedan carrying Scarlet and her abductor made the turn onto the highway.

The phone rang as he angled out of line and onto the berm, tossing dirt and gravel into the air behind him.

"Beaumont," he answered, skirting around waiting traffic.

"This is Officer Barrow," a familiar voice announced. "What's going on? One minute Dispatch has me en route to The Carolina Grand, and the next minute, I'm told you're in vehicular pursuit of Greg Marten."

"I made both calls to Dispatch," Austin said. "He tricked me, came right into the hotel and took her. They're headed southwest on Highway 17." His truck hit the on-ramp with a growl and shot him up to speed. "They're in his Toyota with a two- or three-minute head start I plan to eliminate."

"We've got his vehicle registration. I'll put a notice out on the car and access cameras along 17 to scan for his license plate."

Austin pushed his truck's engine to its limits, determined not to let Scarlet and her abductor get away.

Soon, a car resembling Greg's appeared.

"I think I see it," he said, nudging the gas pedal lower. "They're passing the Camden exit, heading toward Elizabeth City."

"Copy that."

A caravan of semitrucks appeared on the horizon, stretching down the center lane. He'd barely considered the possibility of the trucks becoming a barrier and obstacle when the sedan began to change lanes, cutting in front of the convoy as Austin drew alongside the second truck from the rear.

When he reached the front of the line, the sedan was gone.

A FORK APPEARED on the highway, dividing one inter-state into two. "Where are we going?" Scarlet asked. "What do I do at the fork?"

She needed information, and she needed a plan.

"Stay right. We'll get off at the next opportunity."

Scarlet used her signal and began sliding across four lanes in a mess of traffic, barely avoiding a cara-van of 18-wheelers. "But where are we going?"

"I don't know."

"What do you mean you don't know?" She pursed her lips, reeling in her temper. "You said we're going to start a life together. Where are we doing that? You have to talk to me."

"How can I trust you?" he snapped. His formerly placid expression suddenly filled with rage. "After you spent the night with that man? How can I ever trust you?"

She winced, hoping he hadn't somehow seen what they'd done. Like he seemed to see everything else she did.

"I warned you and warned you," he said. "I told you to knock it off or you'd be punished. And it's as if you don't even care!" he screamed. "What is wrong with you?"

Scarlet focused on the road, muscles tight.

Spittle flew from his mouth with each lament, and he pounded his fists against the dashboard.

"I'm sorry," she said, voice wobbling and tears threatening. "Please don't be angry."

"I thought we had a connection," Greg complained. "You called me for help with the system, with your email, with passwords, and I helped you. I thought we bonded. We got to know one another. You even helped me pick out our house."

"You bought a house?"

His glare burned the skin of her cheek. "I bought the one you told me was perfect for a new family. One that could grow with me."

Her stomach dropped, and the severity of her situation grew infinitely clearer. She remembered the conversation about the house. She'd encouraged him to buy the bigger home, because he had his eye on someone special and hoped to settle down. Maybe start a family.

Greg's expression became affronted, and his mouth set into a grimace. "I can't believe you don't remember."

"I do," she croaked. Suddenly, she saw all those innocent chats with a stranger at the corporate help desk in a drastically different light. And she couldn't help wondering if all her computer issues had really been a result of the new system, or if they'd happened at his hand and by his design, so she'd have to keep calling.

"You said I was your hero," he whispered. "And I believed you."

Heat climbed Scarlet's neck, and nausea rolled in the pit of her stomach. She struggled to breathe, certain she'd be sick or black out and kill them all in traffic. She'd been so thankful for Greg's help every time. She might've even been flirty. And he was right, after a particularly frustrating issue with her email password, she'd called him her hero.

Had that been his tipping point?

"I saved you before, and I'm saving you now," he said, voice lighter. "You see the kinds of choices you make on your own. How easily someone can get to you. Harm you." He lifted the gun from his lap, as if she could've forgotten it was there. "I'm going to keep you safe. You just have to stop fighting me. I can make you happy."

She made eye contact with another driver as she reached the far right lane. The other driver pulled swiftly ahead. A hundred witnesses and no one saw anything, when it felt as if the entire car should be flashing with her distress. Why couldn't others see the dark cloud preparing to consume her?

Greg's hand landed on her thigh again, and her stomach pitched. "Take this exit."

Rolling fields of grass spread into the distance. A forest rose on the right.

Her foot eased off the pedal a bit, not ready to leave the safety of a hundred moving cars.

He pointed his gun into the back seat again, and she took the exit to nowhere.

They rolled along the curving county route with no homes or businesses in sight, and infinite reasons not to go any farther.

Left without options, she burst into a dramatic round of tears. She was out of time for making a good plan, so she'd have to improvise and settle for making any plan and hoping it worked.

Since he seemed hung up on being her hero, tears felt like a good start.

She breathed harder and faster, making each puff audible, and shuddered. Then she pulled onto the side of the road with a series of desperate sobs.

There weren't any cameras to find them here. No passing vehicles to notice they'd stopped. Just them and a whole lot of nature. So she'd focus on getting him out of the car. Then she could drive away with her mom in the trunk and not stop until she found a police station.

"What are you doing?" he demanded. "Drive!"

"I can't," she cried. "I can't. I can't." The tears ran freely now, her true emotions mixing with the show. "Help me. Please!"

Greg swiveled on his seat, looking through the rear window then back to her. "What's wrong? What do you want me to do?"

"You have to drive. I'm shaking. I'll crash if I keep going. I'm—" she considered her believable options "—I think I'm having a panic attack." She shifted into Park and pressed her palms against her face, hoping to make her skin redder, eyes puffier and her overall look more unwell.

"What do you need?" he asked. "A paper bag? Water?"

"Just drive," she said. "I can't do it."

A long beat of silence passed before he spoke again, distrust evident in his voice. "I know what you're doing."

Scarlet steeled her resolve, unfastened her safety belt and reached for him across the armrest.

It was possible he'd take a shot at the car after

he climbed out and she drove away. Possible a bullet would hit the trunk. But at least if that happened, she'd already be in motion, able to find a hospital for her mother. She had to take the risk, because staying with him was a death sentence.

"You're still my hero," she whispered, swallowing bile that rose with the words. "Help me. Please."

Slowly, his tense muscles relaxed beneath her hands, and he pressed his gun-free palm against her back. "Shh," he cooed. "Breathe."

The shudders of repulsion that followed seemed to convince him she truly wasn't in any shape to drive.

"Okay," he said. "But no one's getting out of the car to make this switch. We'll have to slide across the seat to trade places." He pushed the armrests up, creating a flat bench between them, and patted the space.

Scarlet released him, heart thundering, mind racing. She couldn't actually let him drive. He'd have all the control.

Greg scooted into the center of the seat and swung one foot into the well beside hers. "Come on."

She turned and rose, attempting to awkwardly climb over him, but he caught her hips and drew her onto his lap in a straddle. Gooseflesh crawled over her arms like a thousand baby spiders and another hard round of shivers racked her form. She dropped her hands to her sides.

"Hey," he said softly, peering into her eyes. "I've got you." The handle of his gun pressed against her left thigh.

Something heavy registered inside her jacket pocket

on the right. An impossible thought rose in her mind, a tiny sliver of hope.

She maintained eye contact with Greg as she felt the cylindrical shape with her fingertips, then slid her hand into the pocket.

Austin had given her the Taser.

Chapter Twenty-Six

Scarlet wet her lips in concentration as she located the narrow switch at the bottom of the stun gun and slid it into the on position as Austin had shown her. Then she pushed the slider along the device's side to arm it. Now she'd have to choose her moment and be quick.

Greg's gaze moved to her mouth, and his hand skimmed her ribs, apparently misinterpreting her still exterior as submission. He leaned in for a kiss, and she let her head fall to the side, allowing him to access her neck instead.

Ignoring the nauseating feel of his lips on her skin, she gripped the compact stun gun and rested her thumb on the button. When Greg finally sought her mouth, eyelids at half-mast and an eager expression on his face, she thrust forward, connecting her forehead with his. The teeth-rattling collision drew a shout from her captor. His hands flew to his forehead.

The gun's barrel angled toward the roof.

Scarlet squinted against the pain and grabbed his raised wrist, holding the handgun in place while she pressed the stun gun to his neck.

A sickening crackle carved the air, and Greg's gun went off in a burst. The bullet ripped a hole through the roof before his hand opened and the weapon toppled into the back seat.

Scarlet grabbed the keys and threw herself toward the passenger door.

He sputtered and roared, fingers clutching at her shirt as she scrambled away.

She pressed the trunk release button on the key fob, and the lid swung open.

The car rocked as Greg raged, pounding a hand against something inside.

Her mother's curled form came into view as Scarlet reached the trunk.

Trina blinked against the sun. Her usually perfect hair and makeup were in unprecedented ruin. Her skin was pale, and a large bruise marred her cheek. "Scarlet!"

"We've got to go," she said, reaching for her mom.

The driver's door opened, and Greg bumbled into the grass, still spewing horrific strings of swears and clutching a palm to his neck.

"Stay back," Scarlet warned, releasing her mother in favor of resetting her stun gun. "Stay away from us."

Trina wobbled at her side, shaken but alive, then clutched her daughter's arm for balance.

Their assailant glared as he yanked open the door to the back seat. "Oh, I'm going to stay far away from you now. I'm done trying to set you straight. So it's time to end this instead." He stretched inside, and Scarlet spun away, pulling her mother with her.

"Run!" she cried, and the women headed for the trees.

Trina struggled to keep up with Scarlet, despite the fact that she was in far better shape.

Scarlet added that to her ever-growing list of concerns.

"Come on, Mom," she panted. "Just a little farther." They had to make it into the trees before Greg. "We need to find somewhere to hide."

Soon, shade poured over them, and a small measure of relief set in. The forest stretched in three directions, providing plenty of options for cover.

"Here," Trina rasped, pulling her daughter sideways. She ducked behind the broad trunk of a moss-drenched oak then doubled over to vomit on the forest floor.

"Oh, my goodness." Scarlet crouched at her side. "Are you okay?"

"I think I have a concussion," she said, sliding down to sit in the leaves and dirt. "I can't keep running. My head is pounding and spinning. It might explode, if I don't straight-up collapse."

Scarlet pressed a gentle palm to her mother's sweaty face. They couldn't stay there long. They'd be sitting ducks if they didn't keep moving. "How long were you in the trunk?"

"I don't know. Hours maybe," she said. "I was attacked outside my morning showing. I don't even know if that was today. I woke up in a trunk."

Scarlet smoothed her mom's hair away from her eyes. "That was yesterday."

"Scar-let!" Greg's voice echoed through the trees.

He broke her name into syllables and sang them like a nursery rhyme. "You can't hide from me, Scarlet," he taunted. "Don't you know that by now?"

She pressed a finger to her lips, and the women became still as statues.

Leaves crunched and twigs snapped in the distance.

Scarlet held her breath as she peeked around the ancient tree.

Greg was visible through a dense thicket of brush and patch of evergreens. He scanned the forest in the opposite direction.

Her mother tugged her arm then pointed away. A massive boulder stood near the tree line. "Do you still have the car keys?"

She nodded. If they could get to the boulder, they could take another break for Trina's sake then make a run for the car.

She locked eyes with her mother, and Trina stood on trembling legs. Scarlet used her fingers to count to three.

They burst into crouched runs, darting toward the massive stone.

Maniacal laughter erupted behind them. "There you are!" Greg jeered. "No need to bother running now. I've found you, and it's time for your punishment."

The earsplitting crack of a gunshot sent birds into flight from the treetops.

And her mother fell to the ground.

AUSTIN EXITED THE HIGHWAY, certain the sedan must've done the same. He'd only lost sight of it for a few seconds, and it had to have gone somewhere. He slowed to consider his options, which were few. He could return to the highway, but if they were there, his detour would've afforded them a more than generous lead, one he'd likely never make up. Or he could continue on the winding country road, hoping to catch them, assuming they had gotten off the interstate.

Another set of questions crowded into mind before he could sort the last. If Scarlet and Greg had taken the rural exit as suspected, where were they now? And where were they going? According to the big green signs at the bottom of the ramp, the nearest town was twelve miles away. The nearest town with a population over a thousand was nearly fifty miles farther.

A gunshot broke the silence, and Austin went on alert. His truck rocketed forward as he listened carefully for another round of gunfire to break the silence. And he prayed he wouldn't discover a fatality along the roadside. He redialed Officer Barrow.

"What do you know, Beaumont?" the cop asked, answering on the first ring.

"I'm heading east on a county route off exit 113. There's been a shot fired."

"Any sign of the cause?" Barrow asked.

"Not yet," Austin said, floating around the next curve.

Greg's sedan appeared as the road straightened. Trunk lid up. Three doors open.

"I've got eyes on the sedan. Two miles east of the exit. I'm approaching now."

Austin skidded to a stop behind the sedan, and he leaped from the truck's cab, cell phone in one hand, sidearm in the other. "No signs of the passengers."

He turned in a small circle, scanning the scene in all directions. Wondering what to make of the abandoned car. Hoping things weren't as bad as they appeared. "I think she got away somehow and made a run for the trees." That was where he'd go if he needed cover and time to make a plan.

"Copy that," Barrow said. "Help's on the way."

Austin pocketed the cell phone and jogged across the field toward the tree line, phone tucked into his back pocket, sidearm in hand.

SCARLET'S EARS RANG, and the breath left her body. She fell to the earth beside her mother, scooping her into shaky arms. "Mom!"

Trina's eyes opened, then shut.

Scarlet scanned her body for a bullet wound, then frantically searched the forest for signs of her shooter. Trina wasn't bleeding, but she also wasn't responding.

Scarlet's world tilted, and tears fell from her eyes as she imagined all the scenarios where they didn't make it out alive. And all the things she wished she'd told her mother long ago. "I'm so sorry," she whispered.

A gut-wrenching wail rose through the forest.

Scarlet froze, unsure what to make of the sound.

Then someone called her name.

She lifted her head, straining to see without being seen. A familiar silhouette came into view. "Austin?"

"Scarlet!"

She stretched onto her feet and ran to meet him, careful to watch for signs of the shooter.

Austin caught her in his embrace and cupped her face in his hands. "You're okay," he said, stroking her head and holding her tight. "I thought I'd lost you. I don't ever want to lose you."

Emotion clogged her throat and fresh tears stung her eyes. "Mom's hurt, and Greg's got a gun. We have to get her out of here."

Austin shook his head. "I shot Greg and took his weapon. He'll live, but he won't go far. I aimed for his knee."

Scarlet fell against him in relief as sirens wound to life in the distance.

"Let's get your mama," Austin said, and he followed her back to Trina's side.

Chapter Twenty-Seven

Three months later

Scarlet jammed the sale sign into her front yard with equal feelings of relief and remorse. Greg Marten had been charged with multiple counts of assault, attempted murder, abduction, stalking and a bevy of lesser crimes. He'd been convicted of them all. And though she knew, logically, that he'd be behind bars for many years to come, she still felt his eyes on her some days. Especially in places she knew he'd been. Like her beloved waterfront home.

"You okay?" Austin asked, rubbing her shoulders and gazing at the historic cottage he'd tried to help her redeem.

Weekly counseling sessions for her trauma and a thorough cleansing of every room on the property had made a dent in her unease. But she knew now that nothing would fully erase the unsettling sensations she felt there. Not even the brand-new locks and dead bolts had brought her peace.

She raised one gloved hand to cover his. "It's bittersweet," she said, her breath rising on the frigid air in little white clouds. "I love this place, but I can't stay."

"Well," Austin said, moving to stand before her. "How about we go home and get warm? I have a surprise there for you."

"I love everything about those suggestions," she said, curling into his embrace.

He pressed cool lips to her forehead. "Let's go."

The sun was setting as they climbed back into his truck and cranked the heat and defroster. She'd moved the bulk of her regular-use items to Austin's house weeks before, and the Beaumonts had helped her transport the last of her other things into storage last weekend. Now all that was left to do was sell her home.

She peeled off her gloves and held her icy hands in front of the hot air vent. "I hope your surprise involves a fire, a glass of wine and lots of naked cuddling with my favorite human."

"Please let that be me," he said breathlessly.

Scarlet laughed and leaned closer, planting a kiss on his handsome face. "Take me home, Mr. Beaumont."

The drive to Austin's place was borderline perilous in the winter. An exceptionally cold snap had created ice in the ruts and grooves before the covered bridge. Driveway repair would be top priority come spring, or she'd be stuck there permanently.

"What on earth?" she asked, tipping forward as an abundance of twinkle lights became visible on the bridge and in a number of surrounding trees.

Someone had also lined the road with candles burning inside canning jars.

"Do you like it?" he asked.

"I love it! Can we get out? Is this the surprise?"

Austin chuckled and rolled on.

Scarlet twisted on her seat, seeking the beautiful lights and making plans to take photographs from his deck when they got home.

A collection of 4x4s had gathered in the parking space outside the mill.

"Is this a party?" she asked, recognizing a few of the vehicles as belonging to his family. "Or just dinner?" She could never be sure with his family. There were just so many of them, and they gathered for any reason.

Austin parked then turned to grin at her in the darkness. "I'm hoping it's a celebration."

She narrowed suspicious eyes on him. "What are we celebrating?"

"Us." Austin leaned in her direction and kissed her absolutely senseless.

The porch lights flashed on, and Scarlet took a moment to regain her composure.

Hopefully partygoers weren't planning to stay long. She had plans for snuggling that couldn't be ignored.

Mrs. Beaumont waved one arm overhead on Austin's front step. A wool cape clasped around her shoulders. "Come in!" she called, her words muffled through the glass. "It's cold! What are you doing?"

Austin ran the pad of one thumb across his bottom lip, returning her gaze to what she was missing. "Ready?"

Oh, she was ready. Not necessarily for a party, but she would like to see the Beaumonts. Austin's family had embraced her as one of their own, and she loved every encounter. She especially looked forward to his mother's hugs and his brothers' banter. And she deeply appreciated her new sort-of sister too, Dean's fiancée, Nicole.

Scarlet opened her truck door and slid into the cold. Austin met her with a kiss on her nose.

"Finally," his mama said, greeting them with hugs before ushering them inside.

The air smelled of cinnamon and vanilla. Merry chatter rattled down from the second floor.

"Hurry up," Mrs. Beaumont pushed, nudging them toward the stairs. "Everyone's waiting."

Austin took Scarlet's hand and escorted her to the party.

A round of cheers erupted as they reached the little crowd. At least two dozen people raised their glasses. Dean and Nicole, Mr. Beaumont and Finn. Lincoln and Josie, the stable manager at the family ranch. Plus a fully recovered Lydia and Scarlet's mother, to name a few.

"Mom?" She moved in Trina's direction and pulled her into an embrace. The time they'd spent in the forest together had sparked a sort of healing between them that had been long overdue. "What are you doing here?" she asked, grateful and downright shocked to see her outside Holbrook on a work night. Then she remembered the treacherous road. "How did you manage it?"

"Wisely," Trina said, answering the latter question first. "I left my car at the Coulter office in town, and I rode here with Lydia and Finn."

Lydia beamed at Trina's side. The pair had formed a bond in the days since their ugly run-ins with Greg Marten. "Hi, Scarlet. Austin."

Austin shook the ladies' hands.

"Thank you for being here," Scarlet said. "I had no idea we were having a party, or I would've invited you myself." She turned to pin Austin with a playful look of reproach and found him pulling a small velvet box from his pocket.

"It's happening!" Mrs. Beaumont yelled.

Austin laughed, and a hush rolled over their guests. "Scarlet," he said, voice warm and thick with his sexy southern drawl.

"What are you doing?" she whispered, staring at the box and certain she must be wrong.

"I love you," he said. "I was lost for you the moment you walked into my office, and I just keep falling a little further every day you're around. You are strong and smart. Steadfast and sexy."

The crowd chuckled, and Mrs. Beaumont covered her mouth with obvious delight.

"I can't imagine my life without you in it," he said. "And I don't want to. I hope you feel the same way."

"I do." She nodded, head and heart so light she could blow away.

His eyes misted with emotion as he opened the little box and lowered to one knee. "Marry me," he pleaded.

Hot tears swiveled over Scarlet's cheeks as she pulled him up to kiss her.

Then she said yes.

* * * * *

If you missed the first title in Julie Anne Lindsey's
Beaumont Brothers Justice miniseries,
look for Closing In On Clues,
available now wherever
Harlequin Intrigue books are sold!

COMING NEXT MONTH FROM

(H) HARLEQUIN

INTRIGUE

HICNM1123

Get 3 FREE REWARDS!

We'll send you 2 FREE Books plus a FREE Mystery Gift.

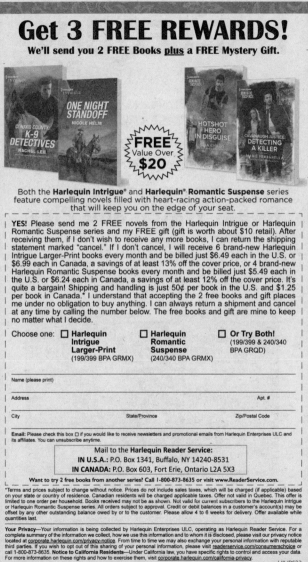

FREE Value Over **$20**

Both the **Harlequin Intrigue®** and **Harlequin® Romantic Suspense** series feature compelling novels filled with heart-racing action-packed romance that will keep you on the edge of your seat.

YES! Please send me 2 FREE novels from the Harlequin Intrigue or Harlequin Romantic Suspense series and my FREE gift (gift is worth about $10 retail). After receiving them, if I don't wish to receive any more books, I can return the shipping statement marked "cancel." If I don't cancel, I will receive 6 brand-new Harlequin Intrigue Larger-Print books every month and be billed just $6.49 each in the U.S. or $6.99 each in Canada, a savings of at least 13% off the cover price, or 4 brand-new Harlequin Romantic Suspense books every month and be billed just $5.49 each in the U.S. or $6.24 each in Canada, a savings of at least 12% off the cover price. It's quite a bargain! Shipping and handling is just 50¢ per book in the U.S. and $1.25 per book in Canada.* I understand that accepting the 2 free books and gift places me under no obligation to buy anything. I can always return a shipment and cancel at any time by calling the number below. The free books and gift are mine to keep no matter what I decide.

Choose one: ☐ **Harlequin Intrigue Larger-Print** (199/399 BPA GRMX)   ☐ **Harlequin Romantic Suspense** (240/340 BPA GRMX)   ☐ **Or Try Both!** (199/399 & 240/340 BPA GRQD)

Name (please print)

Address   Apt. #

City   State/Province   Zip/Postal Code

Email: Please check this box ☐ if you would like to receive newsletters and promotional emails from Harlequin Enterprises ULC and its affiliates. You can unsubscribe anytime.

Mail to the **Harlequin Reader Service:**
IN U.S.A.: P.O. Box 1341, Buffalo, NY 14240-8531
IN CANADA: P.O. Box 603, Fort Erie, Ontario L2A 5X3

Want to try 2 free books from another series! Call 1-800-873-8635 or visit www.ReaderService.com.

*Terms and prices subject to change without notice. Prices do not include sales taxes, which will be charged (if applicable) based on your state or country of residence. Canadian residents will be charged applicable taxes. Offer not valid in Quebec. This offer is limited to one order per household. Books received may not be as shown. Not valid for current subscribers to the Harlequin Intrigue or Harlequin Romantic Suspense series. All orders subject to approval. Credit or debit balances in a customer's account(s) may be offset by any other outstanding balance owed by or to the customer. Please allow 4 to 6 weeks for delivery. Offer available while quantities last.

Your Privacy—Your information is being collected by Harlequin Enterprises ULC, operating as Harlequin Reader Service. For a complete summary of the information we collect, how we use this information and to whom it is disclosed, please visit our privacy notice located at corporate.harlequin.com/privacy-notice. From time to time we may also exchange your personal information with reputable third parties. If you wish to opt out of this sharing of your personal information, please visit readerservice.com/consumerschoice or call 1-800-873-8635. **Notice to California Residents**—Under California law, you have specific rights to control and access your data. For more information on these rights and how to exercise them, visit corporate.harlequin.com/california-privacy.

HIHRS23

HARLEQUIN
PLUS

Try the best multimedia
subscription service for romance
readers like you!

Read, Watch and Play.

Experience the easiest way to get
the romance content you crave.

Start your **FREE TRIAL** at
<u>www.harlequinplus.com/freetrial</u>.